Yeet Me in St. Louis

Crime Fiction from Under the Arch

Edited by

Sandra Murphy

White City

Press

Ten Devilish Tales of Crime and Deception

FROM HAY TO ETERNITY

SANDRA MURPHY

From Hay to Eternity

Here are 10 tales with a twist. The unlikely characters have one thing in common — they're ready and willing to do whatever it takes to achieve their goals.

From a quirky inventor, humored by his neighbors, to two old men out to dinner, to a more-than-meets-the-eye beverage maker, the stories will take you into the minds of the overlooked and unseen. Ignore them at your own risk.

Available in ebook, paperback and audiobook.

Available from https://whitecitypress.com/product/from-hay-to-eternity-by-sandra-murphy/

Yeet Me in St. Louis

Crime Fiction from Under the Arch

Edited by

Sandra Murphy

This edition published by White City Press

An imprint of Misti Media LLC

https://whitecitypress.com

Available in both Paperback and eBook Editions

1 2 3 4 5 6 7 8 9 10

Copyright Respective Authors and Artists © 2024

Paperback ISBN: 9781963479607

eBook ISBN: 9781963479591

Contents

Yeet...

...is a versatile American slang term that can be used as a verb or an exclamation.

Verb: To throw something forcefully, often with enthusiasm, or without regard for the thing being thrown. For example, "He just grabbed my phone and yeeted it into the river."

Exclamation: To express excitement, approval, surprise, or all-around energy. For example, "Yeet!" is often used when doing a dance move or throwing something.

The term became popular in 2014 after being used in dance videos on Black social media and in a Vine video. It was also adopted by online gamers, such as those playing Fortnite, for certain powerful moves. In 2020, "yeet" had a breakthrough during a Saturday Night Live skit starring Pete Davidson and Timothée Chalamet.

Introduction

Here's a bit of St. Louis trivia. Soulard Farmer's Market, built in 1779, is the oldest and largest market west of the Mississippi River. Forest Park, formed in 1876, at 1,330 acres, is one of the largest urban parks in the United States, bigger than New York's Central Park, and attracts more than 12 million visitors a year. The St. Louis Zoo is ranked ninth in the U.S. with over 600 species to visit. Ice cream cones, toasted ravioli, provel cheese, and gooey butter cake are among our food inventions but don't forget a beverage – iced tea and 7up started here. We're big on bbq and beer, with over 65 craft breweries, regional wineries, and award-winning distilleries.

The Arch—we hear a lot of jokes about it but the view is stellar. Each May and September, the lights that illuminate the Arch are turned off to protect migrating birds. If you're afraid you'll be trapped at the top of the Arch, no worries. Each leg has stairs for maintenance workers—1,076 to be exact. It was built to withstand an earthquake. Both the width and height of the Arch are 630 feet. It's the tallest memorial in the United States and the tallest stainless steel monument in the world.

To be included in *Yeet Me in St Louis* there were three must haves—there must be a crime, the setting must be St. Louis, and the Arch must be part of the story. If there was any doubt about the writer being from St. Louis, we had a test—what is provel cheese? All twelve writers are verified St. Louisans.

The stories are as varied as our history, from a cranky two-year-old collector, to mobsters, a threatened cat, or a tour of Black History locations, readers will get a glimpse of what it's like to live in the Gateway to the West.

Eternally young at heart, editor Sandra Murphy has lived in St. Louis for more years than she'll admit. When the smell of hops drift by on a hot summer day, it awakens her imaginary friends who encourage her (force her) to write their stories. Those stories can be found in anthologies published by White City Press and, in her collection, *From Hay to Eternity: Ten Devilish Tales of Crime and Deception.*

Arch Criminals
Eileen Dreyer

In the greater scheme of things, it wasn't a serious crime. It wasn't murder, after all. Not even a bank robbery. But it happened in St. Louis. And in St. Louis, you simply don't steal Stan Musial's ball glove. And you certainly don't do it right before the celebration for the 60th anniversary of his four-hundred-seventy-fifth and final home run hit in his very last game. Especially when it wasn't even the St. Louis Cardinals Hall of Fame's glove, but one his family lent to the team for the celebration.

But on a warm, muggy day in September, that was exactly what happened. Somehow without anybody seeing it, the famed glove simply disappeared from the exhibit case in Ballpark Village to be replaced by a beaten-up old catcher's mitt. Which was how Detective Bridget Scanlon got called away from paperwork involved in a murder investigation. Not a big murder. Just your run-of-the-mill road rage in Jeff-Vanderloo neighborhood where murder wasn't unheard of. They had the perp, they had the weapon, and they had witnesses who would actually testify. They didn't have a motive more than 'he pissed me off', but in this kind of murder, and that kind of neighborhood, it was enough. So Bridget was able to court a sense of completion for a change as she tidied her paperwork before going home. To be honest, Bridget's attention was more on the paramedics from Engine House 5 who were going to meet her in the Grove for drinks, which was how her boss was able to sneak up on her.

"Hey, Red," he said, pushing through the door. "Do I have a gig for you."

Bridget didn't even bother to look up. "I'm going home."

Well. The Chocolate Martini Bar. Close enough.

He plopped himself down on the corner of her desk, right by her bobblehead of Yadi Molina. So, really, it was understandable the Captain would think she'd be delighted to chase this one. He flicked the bobble and sent it nodding in her direction before laying a battered old baseball glove on her desk.

"You'll be a hero to Cardinal Nation," he coaxed.

She grinned, still not looking up from the pile of forms she was tidying. "Don't be silly. I couldn't hit a home run to save my life. Besides, I'd never pass the physical."

"Then I suppose you don't want to know that Stan Musial's baseball glove has been stolen from the Hall of Fame Museum."

As much as she wanted to resist the temptation, that information got her head up to see her boss grin at her. That grin would have scared the crap out of anybody else. It wasn't that he wasn't happy, although he wasn't. He was a thick block of a man with gleaming black skin, shining white teeth, and crinkly pale green eyes that made the rest look kind of otherworldly. And that was before you took in the even shinier bald head that looked piratical, the preternaturally long ears, and the old Marine Corps tattoo barely visible on his neck where it rose out of the crisp lines of his white shirt, red tie, and black suit.

She knew he wanted her to ask about the glove, but she wasn't going to give him the satisfaction.

Leaning back in her creaking chair, Bridget scowled. "Did somebody get murdered for it?"

"Nope. Opened the plexiglass and snuck off like a Dodger." His grin demanded fellow feeling for the bad pun as he pointed to the glove he'd brought with him. "Left this one behind."

Bridget gave her head a slow shake. "If there was no murder, then it isn't my jurisdiction."

"You won't even do it for Stan?"

"I don't think Stan will care. He doesn't play much anymore anyway."

"It's a slam dunk."

"I have a date tonight."

His laugh sounded like the bark of a Great Dane. "No ya don't. C'mon. Not only do I have a theft, but I know where the perp is."

"Then send a uniform to bring them in."

He shook his head. "We know *where* they are. We don't know *who* they are. That's where you come in."

Bridget huffed. "Then bring them all in."

"We're afraid he's gonna dump the glove before we can get to it. We've convinced the people in charge of the site they're to control access and exit."

There was a long silence, punctuated by the sound of computer keys, voices, and at least one 'wah wah' sound from a missed video game.

"Why am I being so blessed?" she demanded.

"Because we have a time crunch on finding that glove, and nobody is more imaginative than you in clearing this shit."

She glared at him. She was afraid he knew she was tempted.

He leaned close. "You can throw out the first pitch next week."

Next week being the first game of the play-offs. Now she knew he knew.

"Not even the Star Spangled Banner?"

The Captain flinched. "Even for Stan's glove, I couldn't traumatize fifty thousand people like that."

She took a minute to stick her paperwork in its folder and entertain a last passing thought for the paramedics, two of whom really liked redheads, Bridget's only distinction.

"All right. Where are they?"

The boss grinned like the Cheshire Cat. "The Arch."

Well, that brought everything to a screeching halt. "The Arch? What do you mean, the Arch?"

He hopped to his feet (a disconcerting sight with his size). She climbed much more slowly to a much shorter height.

"The Hall of Fame security is pretty sure the perp is a member of a church tour group from Utah. There's a minibus-load of 'em, and the bus is sitting in the Arch grounds parking lot."

"Which means they could be anywhere downtown."

"Trust me. They're in the Arch."

Something was fishy in the state of Missouri. "Why don't you get a warrant for the bus?"

"We did. Nothing there."

"So, he stashed it somewhere between Ballpark Village and the van. I wonder where."

"Or if he still has it."

She scowled at him. "I sincerely doubt he was able to shove it down his pants without anybody noticing."

"The odds are admittedly low. Now, c'mon. We can't hold people all night."

She scratched at her neck. "This is about the fact I handcuffed the chief's brother, isn't it? That's why you want me to creak up six hundred feet in one of those freaking claustrophobic eggs so I can play Columbo with a bunch of Bible thumpers."

He had a great line in affronted looks. "Would I do that to you?"

Her grin was dry as a Baptist's living room. "In a minute. Especially if the chief said to."

"But you like the Arch."

"I think it is a majestic monument, an engineering marvel. I don't think it's the place to pick a thief out of a crowd. Especially at the top."

She'd known arguing was a lost cause from the moment he sat his rump down on her desk. She had to make a showing of it anyway.

So she glared. "You owe me."

Even his grin was piratical. "No. You owe me. The chief was pretty pissed."

Bowing to the inevitable, Bridget bent to pull her purse from her desk drawer. "He should be pissed at his brother. He's the one who's been siphoning booze bottles from the bars in Soulard. Why is it my fault that I was in the wrong bar at the wrong time and saw him do it?"

The Captain matched her stride out the door into the hallway. "That's a rhetorical question, right?"

Bridget let loose with another sigh. "Well, it's a good thing I wore my 'I can be mistaken for a tourist' attire today. I'll fit right in. How many people am I bamboozling?"

"They think there are ten people on the tour. Only five men, though. So that should limit the field."

She gave him a glare. "You really have to get over this sexism of yours. Why do you think only men would be interested in a baseball glove? I'd sure be tempted."

He grinned again. "But you're unnatural."

"In St. Louis? Don't be daft. No woman in St. Louis is worth her salt if she can't tell a slugging percentage from a batting average."

And to be fair, she wouldn't at all mind holding onto Stan's glove herself even only as long as it took her to return it to his family.

* * *

Her first hint she might get a little extra help in closing the case came when she reached the front door of headquarters and looked out onto Olive Street to see the wind had kicked up. Litter danced along Olive like snowflakes, and women were holding their skirts down. The sun was still shining, but the light had a weird metallic look to it.

"Oh, that's right," she murmured. She hitched her purse higher and pushed open the door. "We're expecting weather."

"Didn't you drive?" the Captain asked, following her out. "The garage is the other way."

She wasn't paying attention. "Do you know if there are any engineers in our bunch? Especially civil engineers."

The Captain followed the direction of her gaze. There wasn't anything to see, really. Just early fall weather.

"What does that have to do with it?"

"Trust me. Do you know?"

"I do not believe this is a white-collar tour."

She nodded to herself, all but lifted a finger to test the wind. "Good."

Captain looked at her finger. Looked at the skittering paper. Frowned. "What are you thinking?"

She turned her attention to the south-western sky where a low, thick band of black clouds was piling up. They made Bridget smile. Nothing like some natural phenomena to increase tension in the 630-foot-high Arch. She doubted anybody from Utah was well-versed in Midwest weather front. Better yet, with a quick look at the weather radar on her phone and the look of those clouds, especially the ones that would skirt the city to the north, she knew the tornado sirens were about to go off. She couldn't imagine anybody successfully holding onto a pretense of innocence and calm with an imagined tornado bearing down on them.

Usually not something to make Bridget rub her hands in glee but this might just get her to her date.

"If I am not completely confused, I do believe I will be able to breech our thief's defenses."

"How?"

She didn't bother to answer. A unit had just pulled up to the front of the building. Bridget slapped her hand on the hood a couple of times and trotted over to the passenger side.

"Bring me back a souvenir!" the captain demanded.

Bridget gave him a quick wave and ducked into the car.

"The Arch, Jeeves, and make it snappy."

The cop, a veteran of St. Louis streets, just scowled and put the car into gear.

It only took them ten minutes to get to the Arch grounds. It was a lovely place, manicured, green, and leafy with traffic rerouted to a submerged lane so the focus could be lavished on the gleaming steel arch that bisected the sky. Today the trees that lined the greensward twitched in the restless wind.

"You're not about to get off duty, are you, Aranson?" she asked, not taking her attention from the front door to the Arch and its museum.

He scowled. But then, Aranson always scowled. "Midnight."

She nodded. "Then if you can, stay here till I get back with a perp or two."

He took a considered look out the windshield and let go a low whistle. Aranson was a native. He knew what those clouds meant.

Even so, he put the unit in park and turned her way. "You don't want me to come up there with you?"

She slung her purse. "No. I don't want anybody tipped off until I get Stan's glove back."

That got Aranson's attention. "Stan? Musial?"

She nodded. "Somebody up there stole it."

He pulled out a pack of cigarettes and slipped one in his mouth. "Well, why didn't you tell me? Go on. Get up there."

She grinned. "You can keep busy?"

He shrugged. "I have reading to do for sociology class."

That was why Bridget loved people. Aranson looked like a dirt farmer from the Ozarks, pale, lean, as scruffy as a cop could get, dishwater hair and a South St. Louis accent. He didn't wash the car. He warshed it. But she knew he was working on a master's in psychology. It would probably come in handy with a lot of their perps who just happened to be white trash.

Making sure her weapon was covered at her back by her jacket, Bridget climbed out of the car and strode for the front door. The wind picked up a bit, disconcertingly warm and blowing toward the building clouds. Being a St. Louisan, she could read weather radar like a meteorologist. She suspected the danger would go just north of here. There would still be enough noise and wind to cause the effect she wanted, maybe enough to get her to her date after all.

Pulling open the heavy glass doors, Bridget gave a covert flash of her badge to the security guard near the tram doors. "Hear you have some party guests here. Can I get up to see them? Spread a little good cheer?"

The security guard, whose nametag said he was Walters, had a grizzled grin and a hand that rested on his pistol as if it were his best friend. "Right this way, ma'am. We thought if you can say you were in the stairwell they wouldn't know you shouldn't be there."

"The stairwell? What would I be doing there?"

He shrugged. "Studying the engineering? Avoiding the handsy preacher?"

She nodded, following him to the door to the capsule train that would take her up.

"Were you on the metal detector?" When he nodded, she nodded back. "Did you happen to see a baseball glove?"

He shrugged. "Sure. In a black backpack."

"That the only one?"

"As far as I know."

"Who had the backpack?"

Again with the shrug. "Who knows? They all came through in a jumble, picking up a bunch on the way by."

Beside him the door opened. "You'll stop just short of the top," he said, holding it open. "That all right?"

"Sure. By the way, word to the wise. Tornado siren's gonna go off soon. How long after that can you hold the elevator up? The worst of the storm should go north." As it usually did these days.

The security guard rubbed at the graying beard that rimmed his less than square jaw. "Not very long, I'm afraid. Let's coordinate phones and I can keep an ear on you."

She nodded and pulled hers out to coordinate with his. "The magic word for sending the cavalry is Carpenter. Start the capsules again at...oh, toasted ravioli."

She should have said something that was not food. Now she was hungry. She wondered if the paramedics would like to hit a restaurant after the martinis.

Just as she predicted, just as she curled herself into the little egg-shaped cable car that would take her to the top of the Arch, she caught the rising wail of the first tornado siren. Quickly checking her phone, she also found that—again, as she predicted—the most dangerous part of the storm was going to go north of Downtown. It still sounded bad.

When she unwound from the carrier at the top and walked up into the curving floor of the top of the Arch, she realized one of the benefits of being up that high was that you couldn't hear sirens six hundred feet below. The real stress was still coming.

There were a good dozen people milling around, most of them leaning over the windows that stretched along either side of the top and pointed mostly down to get the best panoramic view of St. Louis's busy skyline and East St. Louis's mostly desolate ruin. And, of course, running between, the wide grey ribbon of the Mississippi as it passed beneath. Most times, the people were divided between the windows on both sides. Today, they all seemed to want to look out toward the west. No question why. The sky was dramatic as hell. Sharp afternoon blue bisected with roiling clouds that flickered with lightning. But without hearing the siren, the danger was still theoretical.

Black backpack, Bridget thought, scanning the group of five men, four women and three kids, all meandering except for a little girl who sat on the floor tucked against the metal wall. Pale kid, big eyes. She had a black backpack. So did the man a couple feet away, a beefy guy of about forty with a pornstache and Utah ballcap who was clutching a backpack to his chest.

A black backpack.

Bridget was about to get excited until she looked around. Well, hell. Every damn person up here had a black backpack. All being clutched like unhappy babies.

But the guy with the stache had a Cardinals shirt on. Maybe that meant....

Three other people turned around to show identical red t-shirts beneath jackets and light sweaters. So, not so easy. Even two of the kids had Cardinals' shirts on.

She was still in luck. Nobody was really paying attention to her. Still clutching their backpacks, they seemed mesmerized by the approaching weather. One of the security guards sidled over to Bridget and nodded.

"Anything?" she asked.

"No'm. Seems a normal group."

All with black backpacks and most with Cardinal shirts. And looking just a weensy bit apprehensive. Although if she were from anyplace but St. Louis, Bridget knew she'd be a little apprehensive herself at the sight through those windows.

It got a lot more tense when Bridget's phone let off the ominous tones of an alert.

"Weather advisory," the sharp voice announced as she pulled the phone from her pocket. "A tornado warning has been issued for the city and county of St. Louis. Seek shelter immediately. Stay away from windows...."

Every eye was on her now. People were snapping to attention, eyes swiveling as if they were watching a tennis match.

"We need to get down," one plump blonde lady in a flowered dress cried.

"I'm afraid the electrical problem is still being fixed, ma'am," the security guard said.

Bridget took her own surreptitious look out the western windows and began to count. Shouldn't be too long now....

And there it was, the first blast of wind that presaged a big weather front. You didn't just hear it up here, like a groan, you felt it. The Arch swayed under their feet.

Everybody froze.

"Wow," Bridget murmured, stepping closer. "Sure hope we get down soon."

Two, three, and another blast. Another minimal sway that was perfectly normal unless you were from Utah, where the tallest thing in the state was probably the Mormon Temple.

Everybody moved, milling around like cows in a storm. Bridget watched, but even the backpacks weren't a help. Nobody was setting off her alarms. One carrier was a thin, bespeckled guy with big teeth and a habit of patting the woman with him on her shoulder. One of the women, just about the only one not wearing the team t-shirt, kept looking back and forth as if planning an escape. No backpack, though. Another fiftyish man with a well-trimmed brown beard had a backpack he accidently bumped against a sharp-faced brunette woman with blue nails and a khaki carryall.

"We could walk down," somebody suggested, their voice a little thin and high.

Bridget shrugged. "That's a lotta steps."

Good heavens, three more people had backpacks. She wasn't going to have enough time to sweet talk these people into offering up that glove. The wind buffeted them again and at least two people groaned. She thought one of them started to pray.

"I can't wait to get down," she said to the stache guy. "I want to know what happened over at the stadium."

He turned toward her and she saw one of his teeth was gold. "The stadium? What about the stadium? We were just there."

"I don't know. Lots of cops over by the Hall of Fame. One of 'em said something about a robbery."

Okay, she wasn't being subtle but the captain had been right. They didn't have a lot of time. Besides, she did get some reaction. One furtive look at a button-down lady from the stache guy. A clutching of a backpack from the skinny guy, who seemed to be in charge. Well, maybe not in charge. He at least had the biggest backpack. And he was holding onto it like purloined treasure. He was also patting a nervous gray-haired ancient who muttered about the one time she had been caught in a tornado. Nope. Not who she wanted. She wasn't feeling comfortable naming any of them.

The reason the Cap sent her was because she had a sense for these things. She had a knack. Cap often claimed she could smell a perp in a crowd. She smelled nothing.

Then the lady with the blue nails made the tiniest gesture. She bent over the little girl who sat curled up against the arced metal wall. She bent over and tapped the black backpack in the little girl's arms. And then, smiling, she laid those blue-nailed fingers against that little girl's cheek, and the girl smiled. Just that.

And Bridget wanted to spit.

Because she saw. Just as the wind gave the Arch another impatient push, she realized she had been looking for hidden clues, when the truth was sitting there all along, out of the way, silent. Pale and thin with circles under her eyes and long sleeves in summer. Long sleeves on a Cardinals' shirt.

"Boy," she said, hands in pockets, "I could sure use some toasted ravioli right about now."

The lady with the nails smiled. "I hear that's good."

Bridget nodded. "The best."

"Ladies and gentlemen," the security guard announced, "if you line up for the tram down, we're ready to go."

Bridget stepped up to the blue-nailed lady and the little girl. The lady reached down to take the bag from the girl, but the little one shook her head. She held out a hand. The lady took hold as if it would too easily shatter, and the little girl grimaced. She made it to her feet and then wobbled.

Bridget instinctively reached over to steady her. "Cardinals fan?" she asked.

The little girl offered a small smile. "My dad loves them. We came for him."

Bridget looked up at the blue-nailed lady, who suddenly looked strained. "He's home in Utah," she said, anchoring the girl against her side. "He wasn't well enough to come."

Bridget smiled at them both. "So you made the pilgrimage for him."

The little girl smiled. She took a step and then lurched against Bridget.

Bridget lent a hand. "A little shaky yourself," she offered.

The woman must be the girl's mother. She wrapped her arm around the girl's shoulder. "Make a Wish gave us the chance to come."

Which meant the stakes had just changed. Fortunately, Bridget Scanlon was known for being able to think fast on her feet.

* * *

It was the next morning when the city sparkled all clean and new after the series of storms had swept through the night before and steam curled up from the humid streets that Detective Bridget Scanlon had her next visit from her captain. She was at her desk typing up an interview she'd done on a case that involved gangs, drugs, and revenge when Yadi's head began to once again bob and her desk shifted under the Captain's weight.

"What did you do, Scanlon?"

She didn't even look up. "Why, I didn't do anything, Cap."

He leaned in. "Don't give me that bullshit. Why is Musial's glove back in place when I don't have a robbery suspect on my sheet?"

This time she did look up, offering him her patented innocent look. "Robbery? What robbery?"

"Precisely. I sent you to do a job, Scanlon. It is only half accomplished. Why is that?"

"Is the Musial family happy?"

His scowl was impressive. "They are."

"Is the glove on display?"

This time the scowl involved growling. "You know damn well it is. But I sent you to bring back a suspect, and even Aranson is acting like I hallucinated the whole thing. I need an explanation before I bust you to housekeeping."

Bridget bowed back to her work. "Well, I don't know about that, Cap. I do know I met the most lovely little girl named Emmy yesterday who was given a chance to see her favorite ballclub—and her father's—through the Make a Wish Foundation, even though she is in the middle of chemotherapy. What she really wanted was to make her father happy. You see, he's back in Utah waiting for a heart so he can have a transplant. So she was hoping to find a way to make him happy."

There was a long pause. "Don't tell me. His favorite Cardinal is Stan

13

Musial."

She smiled up at him. "You're a psychic, Cap. All that little girl could talk about was lending her father something to take his mind off his problems. She loves her father a lot, you know."

"Lending."

She nodded over her paperwork. "Her mom thinks the ordeal he'd need some emotional support for would only be for a little while."

Which the Cap interpreted quite accurately enough to give into a resigned sigh.

"But the glove is back, Scanlon. How does that happen?"

"You know St. Louis, Cap. It's not just what you know. It's who ya know."

That produced a growl. "And?"

Bridget thought of the glow in the little girl's eyes and smiled again. "Turns out Stan had more than one glove."

The Unrelenting Question
G.R. Miller

The fog in my head cleared. A big man loomed before me, then leaned in again, this time his crooked nose stopped inches from mine. The unnatural twist and scars indicated this guy's schnoz had been the target for a fist more than once. Maybe a heavyweight boxer who never made it past practice dummy for the champ. Garlic and cigarettes tainted the man's breath as he continued his interrogation, "So, I'll ask again. What about today? Did you get it done?"

Bound to a chair with my arms tied behind me, I sat back as far as I could. "Today, tomorrow, next week, next month, next year––like I already told you, man, I don't know what the hell you're talking about."

He reached back and slapped my face with his burly hand. "That jar your memory?"

I blinked and flexed my jaw to see whether it was still attached, then raised my head to an upright position. At least the motor function portion of my brain hadn't been knocked through my ear onto the floor. Unsure what gray matter remained intact, I slowly inhaled, held the air for a few seconds, then let it go.

"Well?" he said.

"I think you belted my memory into oblivion."

"Vivian? Whatta you know about my woman?"

"I said o-bli-vi-on. As in 'To infinity and beyond.'"

He reached back with his other hand. Apparently, the big oaf wasn't a Toy Story fan.

I flinched. "Hold on, pal. Look, I don't know you or your woman. And I damned sure don't know why you've got me in this musty old cellar, bound to a chair. If I knew anything, rather than taking a beating, you can bet your sweet ass I'd be telling you."

The guy grunted, then followed through with a backhanded fist from the opposite direction. The blow knocked me over—chair and all. Evidently annoyed by the Buzz Lightyear reference, guess he didn't care for my sweet ass comment either.

As if the bruiser had turned out my lights, I lay still, eyes closed, with steady but shallow breaths. While trying not to twitch, I concentrated on recreating the moment the bully and I had first met.

He'd coerced me through the side door of a panel van parked at the curb. But what curb? Where were we? What had the big guy said? Who else was in the vehicle? Had any of them said anything to one another?

Further images of my abduction began to come together.

The burly palooka had called the driver Vivian—his woman. Apparently the only other person in the vehicle, Vivian had to have been a co-conspirator in this fiasco. But conspirators in what? Where was she now? Above all, why me? What did I have that they'd want?

Continuing to lie on the dank floor like a road-killed possum, I refocused on the entire abduction scene.

It had been dark out. I'd just left work and was walking to my car when the burly man had approached and taken me hostage. Cars with preoccupied drivers continued to pass by on Seventh Street.

My recollections switched to replaying the dialogue.

Mine was simple. "What the f—?"

Burly Man was the talker-in-charge as he'd grasped my arm. "I've got a gun pointed at your gut. Shut up and get in the van."

Once inside the van he'd said to his cohort, Vivian, "Get us over to the house."

Vivian had turned and acknowledged the command to drive with an odd response, "You mean us and our ticket to the good life, right?" Headlights from a passing vehicle had shined through the van's small rear windows and highlighted her face. Though no youngster, Vivian had appeared rather attractive with big round eyes, a narrow nose, and a pouty lower lip. Had she winked?

I shook off her vision and replayed the duo's last comments.

"Get us over to the house." Followed by, "You mean us and our ticket to the good life, right?"

The house had to be where we were now. But were we still in St. Louis or across the river in Illinois? And how was I anybody's ticket to the good life? Then I remembered Burly asking me for the first time, "What about today? Did you get it done?"

Burly had repeated the same damned questions at least a half-dozen times as we'd weaved through downtown traffic. My persistent dumbfounded replies must have tried his patience. He'd growled and then stabbed me with a syringe. The world quickly went black.

Next thing I knew, I was in this musty cellar, bound to a chair.

Still portraying the comatose victim on the floor, I listened for movement. Burly huffed a few times in frustration, then kicked my knee and waited. When I failed to respond, he spit in my direction and then clomped up the stairs.

Once the door slammed, I sighed––no, more like whimpered. Damn that hurt! Based on the ache in my knee, the big bastard's boots had to have steel toes. After the lambasting from both sides, my jaw didn't feel much better than my knee.

Breathing deep and slow, I considered what might have inspired Burly and Vivian to believe I was their path to the good life? I was just one person in a pool of IT techs at…the bank.

"Shit," I whispered. "I thought Henderson was acting weird."

Each IT tech at First Union Bank had access to a system that dealt with money transfers every day. Transfers that, from the right accounts, could amount to millions. My coworker had seemed edgy lately— always looking around the office like a kid ready to stuff both hands into his grandma's cookie jar. I'd asked Henderson about his apparent unease several times, but he'd always insisted everything was okay—

just a few problems at home that he was taking care of.

Now it was obvious how he was going to take care of them.

At six-feet tall, Henderson and I were about the same height and build. Same color hair parted on the same side. Even with bank-issued nametags, our supervisor was constantly confusing the two of us. Said we could be twins. "Dammit."

Burly and his woman began talking upstairs, their exchanges muted by the hardwood floor. In the dim light from an incandescent bulb hanging in the stairwell, I scanned my surroundings. A reflection from across the basement caught my eye. If I moved, Burly and Vivian might hear me. If I did nothing, I'd most likely die.

Conversation from above mellowed, then ceased. Contented moans replaced the chatter followed by the unmistakable rhythm of passion. Apparently, I was beneath the bedroom.

I rolled to my knees, winced, then managed to stand––sort of. Hard to straighten with a chair clinging to your butt. Thank God for Yoga.

Shuffling in time to the lovemaking, I reached the beacon that would hopefully assist my escape––a shattered mirror. After positioning the chair, I carefully felt for an edge of the broken glass. Coordinating my gyrations with my abductors' lustful rhythms, I sliced through the rope that secured my arms behind me. At last, I was free. But trapped in the windowless cellar of an antiquated house, the only way out was up the squeaky stairs. I closed my eyes and began to formulate a plan, one that would surely require patience.

Minutes felt like hours. Burly must have taken testosterone supplements. Or maybe he was a client of one of the increasing numbers of male enhancement clinics. Regardless, the big man's endurance allowed me time to think about how to execute my scheme.

What did Burly mean when he'd asked, "What about today? Did you get it done?" Had Henderson and the rambunctious duo upstairs concocted a plan to defraud the bank? Had Henderson left early today because he'd become afraid of the consequences, decided to back out of the arrangement, and set me up as his look-alike patsy? "That son of a—"

18

The amorous session above finally settled into silence. Moments later, water began to flow through the cast-iron pipes. A few minutes later, while the water continued to flow, the floor creaked, the cellar door opened, and Burly's heavy feet clomped down the wooden treads.

Standing beneath the stairs, I waited for my opportunity. When Burly spotted the empty chair, he started to speak. My cue to react. I reached through the open riser space with both hands, grabbed the big man's boots, and pulled. He gasped, then yelled as he tumbled and thumped to a less-than-graceful, face-first landing. His head cracked against the limestone foundation. Following a monumental groan, he lay limp as an old ragdoll.

The water stopped running and bare feet slapped across the hardwood. Burly Man's semi-automatic handgun had fallen beside him. I snatched the weapon from the sweaty concrete floor and spun toward the cellar doorway.

Burly's woman stood at the top of the stairs. Her wavy dark brown hair draped upon her shoulders. A towel with a picture of the Gateway Arch printed on it barely hid her curvy nakedness.

I aimed the gun in her direction and grinned. My turn to ask the question. "So, Vivian. What about today?"

Arch Rivals
Daniel Sohn

"I don't get it. They tore all this down? For what?" Alphonse Garganelli surveyed more than eighty acres of dirt and rubble along the St. Louis riverfront. He produced a cigar from his three-piece pinstripe. Across the Mississippi, over Illinois, cirrus clouds glowed twilight red.

Tony Coletta struck a match for Mr. Garganelli. "They're puttin' up a monument."

"Yeah? Who tore down my warehouses? How many did I lose?" Garganelli puffed his cigar, and from beneath his fedora, watched Coletta.

"Four." Coletta braced for a tirade.

"But they saved those two." Garganelli gestured with an angry flick of his hand. "The Cathedral. I guess that's okay. But what's the other?"

"That's the Old Rock House," Coletta answered.

Garganelli chewed his cigar. "My warehouses gone for this. Whose rock house is it? I want a piece a that. You hear me, Tony. Get me a piece."

"Yes sir, Mr. Garganelli. We'll have an opportunity when they move it."

"And whose monument? That Finnish fella? What'd ya call it? An Arch? Did we kill him yet?" Garganelli growled.

"No, sir."

"Why not? What are we waitin' for? Time to call in Karmello and Dito."

"Eero Saarinen, the Finn, he's dead already."

"Somebody beat me to it? Prob'ly Egan."

"No, sir. It was a brain tumor. He died in surgery."

"So, a doctor did the job. Get 'is name. Send 'im flowers." Alfonse Garganelli turned away. Dusk stole the fire from the now dark blue clouds.

A bodyguard and driver accompanied Coletta and Garganelli to a black Cadillac Deville. The bodyguard held the car door.

"Where to Mr. G?" the driver asked.

"Gaslight Square. The Golden Eagle," Mr. G replied, then looked at Coletta. "Any news?"

"Our union bosses are managing the monument job," Coletta said.

"Good. Do we have a lock on oversight of the monument once it's opened?" Garganelli asked.

"The mayor is with us and six of the fourteen aldermen. We'll land four more in the upcomin' election. That should set us up."

"Yeah? Okay. Here's the thing. We can't litter the city with stiffs no more. Makes the mayor look bad. Tell Lupo. He's got to have his boys clean up after theirselves." Mr. G slapped the car seat. Coletta jumped but collected himself quickly.

* * *

Three weeks later, the mayor met with Mr. G in a private room at the Golden Eagle. A bottle of grappa and two shot glasses on a mahogany table between them set the tone for business. Above the table, a crystal chandelier sparkled. As he sat, Mr. G felt his shoes slide across the patterned maroon Persian rug.

"Parts of the Old Rock House went missing when it was moved. You wouldn't know anything about that, would you?" The mayor stared at Mr. G as he poured grappa into the glasses.

"What old rock house?"

"Come on, Alphonse. Don't play me. This will cause a lot of trouble. The memorial commission is screaming. They'll be complaining to the President! The US President! It makes St. Louis...and me...look bad."

Mr. G puffed his cigar. "I'll see what I can do, mayor. Might cost me, but we wanna help you. Like you'll help me." They toasted and downed the pomace brandy.

* * *

A few days later, Patrick Egan's hitmen sat at a table outside Peacock Alley. The wide Gaslight Square sidewalks served as patios for seating and strolling, seeing and being seen. "Mad Dog" Coll and "Whitey" Higgins scanned the Gaslight Square traffic, both motorized and on foot, as they cruised by. Mad Dog's large frame overlapped his chair. Whitey's lean, angular appearance belied his fierce grit.

"Garganelli's gang's gonna' be so ragin'," Mad Dog chuckled into his beer.

"It's a beautiful thing. They stole the Rock House pieces to begin with. Now we got 'em," Whitey said.

"Before they could turn 'em back in to keep the mayor happy." They both laughed. "Egan says to lay low though," Mad Dog continued. "He'll finger the Russo gang or the Cuckoos."

The two thugs watched a black Mercury with dark windows cruise slowly toward them. "That's Russo's guys," Whitey said. He slid his right hand into his jacket and gripped his bulldog revolver.

"Whitey, cool it," Mad Dog said. "No gunplay in Gaslight. All the gangs agreed. Fairness of kerns."

"Till someone disagrees." Whitey kept his finger by the trigger. The car slowed, nearly coming to a stop by their table. Whitey sneered and pulled the bulldog from its holster. When the car moved on, he relaxed.

"It'd be too messy anyway. Remember we got new rules. No mortos in the gutter." Mad Dog reminded him.

"Bullshite, i'n it? What are we gonna do with 'em?" They both thought for a while. Whitey ordered another round. "Dumpster?" Whitey snapped his fingers.

"Bullocks. We're supposed to hide 'em. Like so they'll never be found. You'll have the dumpsters stinkin' like bad cabbage." Mad Dog focused on the bubbles rising through his beer.

"Sewer system!" Whitey blurted. "Pull up a manhole cover and make a deposit."

"Crap talk, Whitey! And clog up the sewers?"

"Quit actin' the maggot. I'm thinkin' out loud here. Gimme somethin' besides the jacks." Whitey complained. They both paused, distracted by passing couples dressed for show.

"Bury 'em in vacant lots?" Mad Dog knew this was a bad idea as he said it.

"Yeah. Great. You're the shovel man. Nobody drivin' by will notice, eh?" Whitey gazed after a brunette in a tight red dress.

"I know." Mad Dog leaned forward. "The Big Muddy," he whispered.

Whitey considered how to criticize this idea. "Can't have any floaters."

"Yeah. Tie rocks to 'em and toss 'em off a bridge." Mad Dog took a long drink.

"The bridges are too busy," Whitey said.

"Not at 4:00 a.m. on the 66-bypass bridge."

* * *

The Egan gang had a fierce rivalry with another Irish gang, the Cuckoos. Add on turf battles with the St. Louis Italian gangs and bloodshed occurred every day but Sunday. Less than a week after deciding how to hide their victims, Mad Dog and Whitey had a dead Cuckoo in the trunk of their Pontiac.

"I like the old way better. Leave 'em on the street so people know we mean business." Mad Dog flipped a cigarette out the window. He drove east on the Route 66 bypass highway.

"It's somethin' about the mayor. Citizens stirrin' up a storm about murders in the city. Maybe it'll all blow over," Whitey said.

At 4:15 Monday morning Mad Dog stopped at the toll booth on the Missouri side of the Mississippi river. The gatekeeper startled awake. "Two bits," he said. There were no other cars in sight.

As they drove on to the bridge, Whitey said, "Stop at the bend. We can do the drop there. We'll be outta sight from the toll booth."

"Why's there a bend anyway? I never hearda no bridge changin' directions in the middle of a river," Mad Dog said.

"I dunno. Some eejit went arseways. Here. Stop here." The Pontiac came to a halt just past the bridge's twenty-two-degree angle. Mad Dog switched off the headlights. Whitey jumped out to unlock the trunk. They stood for a moment to listen. The Mississippi sighed at the bridge piers, sending its familiar earthy scents of rotting fish, worms, and plants. Moonlight reflected off the thick river's ripples. The mobsters bent to their heavy task.

"You tied on too much weight," Mad Dog complained. "And look at this railing. It's six feet tall."

"Quit yer whinin'. Ya gettin' soft around the middle?" Whitey and Mad Dog hoisted the burlap wrapped corpse toward the fence top. Mad Dog lost his grip and dropped his end. Weights tied onto the dead man swung down and smacked Whitey's shins.

"What the fook!" Whitey let go of his end. He rubbed his legs. "Grab 'im tight, ya langer! Ready? One, two, three heave." They lifted the body to the top of the fence where finials snagged the burlap. The weighted corpse hung out over the river, hooked on a dozen spikes.

"Damn the Furies," Mad Dog hissed. "Pull up next to the fence"

As Whitey maneuvered the car to the railing, a delivery truck approached from the Illinois side. It slowed then stopped next to the Pontiac.

"Need some help?" The driver called out.

"No," both gangsters yelled.

"Get lost," Whitey called out over his shoulder. The trucker stared, then pulled away.

Whitey and Mad Dog climbed onto the car. With one foot on the roof and one on the fence, they pulled at the burlap, releasing the heavy bundle one finial at a time.

"Damn it, Whitey. I'm sweatin' like a manky scut." As if in response to his complaint, the burlap ripped just below the last three finials. The corpse spilled out of its wrapping, followed by three iron weights.

"Son of a banshee," Whitey cursed. They both watched the body, then the weights, splash into the murky waters far below. The body partially surfaced, then disappeared. "Maybe it'll sink anyway," Whitey said as they yanked the burlap off the pointy fence spikes. Mad Dog made the sign of the cross.

"We gotta take the MacArthur back to the city. That trucker gave us a good look. Shoulda shot 'im," Mad Dog said. Then, giving Whitey a look, added, "Good thing this went so crackin' smooth."

Whitey smirked, "It's fookin' banjaxed. Just hope the dumbass Cuckoo don't get fished out by a water patrol. If Egan finds out…". Whitey felt a shiver as he gazed down river. He again could make out something floating. The body, he thought, with one arm raised out of the water. It appeared to motion at him. Whitey's growing terror was interrupted by Mad Dog.

"Exactly, Whitey. Good thing it all went perfect." Mad Dog accentuated each word. He hadn't noticed Whitey's pale countenance nor the floating form which still gripped Whitey's superstitions.

Whitey looked away from the apparition, hesitated, then said "We gotta get outta here." He felt his hands shake when he slammed the trunk. "I don't care how we do this next time, but I ain't comin' back t'dis bridge. I'd rather dig a hole and jump in it meself."

"No. We ain't startin' no cemetery. But I saw somethin' in the papers. The City's doin' the diggin' for us." Mad Dog revved the engine.

* * *

"You see Alan Ginsburg in Gaslight last week?" Tony Coletta asked Goo Goo Ellison, the Egan gang member who was blackmailing him for being homosexual. Ellison was also gay but feared no reprisals from his gang. They walked along a gravel trail by a bluff.

"Yeah," Goo Goo said. "He's a wild man. He got drunk on wine while doing his show at the Cellar Door."

"No surprise. Did he read from 'Howl'?" Coletta hated being vulnerable to the rival gangster, but knew he was trapped.

"Yeah, and some new works. He read those with a mellow jazz backup. Cool gig. I went to an after-party where Ginsberg brought a Buddhist monk. He's a gay Buddhist, ya' know." Goo Goo sat on a bench by the path. Coletta joined him.

"Wish I coulda been there. Too risky for me. Your people don't care you're a poofter. Mine would kill me if they knew," Coletta lamented. They both considered this as a strong wind blew through the trees.

"Guess it's the difference between Irish Catholics and Roman Catholics. Ireland's got ferries. Rome's got marble statues and monuments. Ya take things too serious," Goo Goo offered. "So, any news for me?" Goo Goo was careful with how he fed Coletta's information to Egan. He didn't want anyone to catch on Tony was his source. Not even Egan.

"Mr. G's heated up over the missin' Rock House pieces. He thinks it's another gang – Russo, the Cuckoos, or you guys. He wants to start goin' after people to beat information out of 'em."

"That's gonna be messy." Goo Goo looked across the Mississippi River valley from Bee Tree Park, their usual meeting spot. "It's risky. Linin' a row of dominos, waitin' for one to tip."

"Yeah. Messy. How can we switch it up?"

"We could get rumors goin' that the Rock House parts were stolen by a Garganelli gang splinter group. Are any of Mr. G's lieutenants clever enough to be suspected?" Goo Goo asked.

"Maybe. Mr. G's suspicious about mosta the gang. That's why he's made it so long. Trapani or Pozzallo are both tough guys with ambition, but it would be better not to name names. Just the rumor of someone makin' a power play is all we need," Coletta said.

"You know Mr. G controls the unions on the Arch job, right?" Coletta asked.

"Yeah. We got a lot of Micks workin' there. It's a good place to start rumors."

* * *

Mr. G sat at his office desk. A cloud of cigar smoke hung over him in the dim light. Dark wood paneling matched his mood. "Lupo, what are you tellin' me? Karmello and Dito can't catch nobody?"

Giuseppe Lupo's face never gave anything away. "No sir, Mr. G. I'm tellin' you the people they asked had nothin' helpful to say."

"Maybe dey didn't ask nice enough," Mr. G growled.

"They don't call Dito 'The Butcher' cuz he asks nice. He and Karmello got the same thing from all three. A Cuckoo, a guy from Russo's gang and one from Egan's. Same as the rumors goin' around."

"That one of my people has the Rock House pieces? I don't believe it."

Lupo stood silent, waiting. He didn't believe it either but knew not to speak.

"Where's Coletta? He knows people."

"I'll tell him he's needed," Lupo said.

Mr. G examined his cigar. "Yeah Lupo. You do that. You tell 'im he's needed."

* * *

Tony Coletta leaned against his convertible in a parking lot by the Arch construction site. He saw Lupo's Hudson Hornet pull in. Coletta stepped forward where he could be seen.

Lupo got out from the back seat. "They tol' me you'd be down here," he said. The two men faced each other like mannequins dressed in grey flannel suits.

"Yeah. Meetin' the union boss. Mr. G wants me to keep tabs here." Coletta motioned with his head.

"Any problems?"

"Nothin' big. We've worked out for Karmello and Dito to make deliveries here. Can't leave 'em on the street no more, but we noticed the nice hole they got over there." Coletta nodded over his shoulder. "Trouble is, Karmello's been too busy lately. The boss here's worried someone will notice."

"How many have they tossed in?" Lupo wondered if he'd lost count.

"Three last week. Don't seem so bad." Coletta shrugged.

"Uh huh. Well, there'll be more coming. You work it out." Lupo paused. "Mr. G wants to see you."

"I'll get with him as soon as I'm finished here. Or should I go now?" Coletta knew Lupo would like the deference. He also knew the answer.

"Get it sorted out with the union boss first." With that, Lupo turned to his car.

Coletta watched as Lupo departed, then walked toward the construction office. There, he stood outside and gazed down at an immense hole six stories deep. Once filled with concrete, it would serve as the base for the north leg of the monument.

He heard steps approaching from behind. "Are you with Garganelli?" Coletta turned to see the union boss. "Oh, hey Tony," he said. "What's goin' on wit' you guys? I got a structure to build that's goin' to end up half fulla dead bodies."

"I only know of three deliveries last week," Coletta said

"Five. The boys told me five. I just don't want no reporters catchin' wind of this. If word gets out, we'll have cops all over the place."

"Five? You're sure?" Coletta narrowed his eyes. Were Karmello and Dito doing some side jobs again? If Lupo found out… "I'll check into it. Last week was unusual. It'll quiet down."

* * *

Patrick Egan paced in a back room of O'Connell's Irish Pub. "Have you two mugs been dumping bodies in the river?" He stopped to glare at Mad Dog and Whitey.

"Just one, Mr. Egan. Couple a weeks ago. Off the Chain a Rocks. But it was tied with weights," Whitey shivered.

"Everything went perfect," Mad Dog added.

"Who saw you do it?" Egan took a drink of Bushmills. His glass met the oak table with an emphatic thump. Whitey broke into a sweat. His mouth cottoned. He could not speak.

After a moment, Mad Dog answered, "No…No one. No witnesses. We were past the bend from the toll house. It was 4:00 a.m. Nobody around."

"The police are investigatin'. Ya best be tellin' me the truth."

"Yes, sir." Mad Dog didn't notice Whitey's agitation. "Anyways, we've worked out a new way, usin' that big hole the city's dug for the Arch. Owney Boyle runs security three nights a week. In the mornin', the cement crews don't see nothin'."

"Owney's not on our payroll. Have him come see me."

"Yes sir, Mr. Egan. We'll tell 'im." The hitmen walked out into the warm evening dusk. Gaslight Square was already crowded along Olive Street.

"Let's stop in at Mosley's. I need a whiskey before we make our delivery," Mad Dog said.

"Yeah. Close shave," Whitey hoped more whiskey would finally purge the wraith visions that continued to plague him.

The whiskey went down smooth until well after midnight. At 3:00 a.m. they pulled into the Arch construction parking lot and cut the headlights. Mad Dog let the Pontiac coast to the back of the lot.

"Let's go, Whitey." He turned off the engine. They stumbled in the gravel but focused on their task.

"Where's Owney?" Whiskey clouded Mad Dog's certainty. "He's usually waitin' around here."

Whitey unlocked the trunk. They pulled out a heavy burlap bundle and carried it to the fence line. Just beyond was the massive hole. The river's scent was mixed with diesel fumes. Mad Dog froze.

"What's a matter? Le's go," Whitey slurred.

"Shhh. 'Ear 'em voices?" They both held their breath, listening. Over the sound of a generator, they heard talk.

"That don't sound like Owney," Whitey whispered. "We gotta make the drop and scram."

"What'r they doin' over there?" Mad Dog could see several people across the pit. "Hey! They just dropped a package into our hole. Is this Thursday? Where's Owney?"

"I don't know. No, wait, it's Wednesday. Owney's not gonna be here. C'mon, let's get this stiff delivered." Whitey grabbed one end of the bundle and started to drag the awkward load.

"Okay, okay, keep it down. We don't know the guard." Mad Dog grabbed the other end. They lifted their victim toward the top of the fence.

Someone shouted from across the abyss. "Hey! Who's there? What d' ya think you're doin'?" Karmello, Dito and an Arch Security man spotted Whitey and Mad Dog.

"They're doin' a drop! In our hole!" Karmello said. They all pulled Colt 19-11 sidearms.

"Quick, lash it." Whitey said, heaving. Just as they pushed the body over the fence and into the pit, shots rang out. They ducked and pulled snub-nose revolvers. Whitey fired towards the men, BAM.

"You'll never hit anything with a Bulldog at this distance," Mad Dog said. Several more shots came from the men across the pit. "They got serious firepower. Colts, by the sound of 'em."

"It'll make 'em think twice though." Whitey fired more rounds in rapid succession, 'BAM, BAM, BAM'. The reports echoed off nearby buildings and up Market Street through downtown St. Louis. A cement truck pulled up on the far side of the pit. Next to it, a light tower switched on.

"They're comin' this way. We better leg it," Mad Dog said. "Where's the car?"

"Over there, I think," Whitey said. He began an unsteady run. Mad Dog lurched after him. More shots rang out. Bullets snapped past, hit nearby gravel, and struck the car's hood.

Mad Dog took the wheel. Whitey fired his last shots, 'BAM, BAM'. The Pontiac roared to life, sprayed gravel, then slammed to a sliding stop. Mad Dog saw the pit's fence close in the headlights. A bullet shattered his window.

"You're goin' the wrong way!" Whitey yelled. He tried to reload but kept dropping bullets. "Gimme your heater!" As Mad Dog maneuvered, Whitey opened his window and began to fire wildly in the general direction of the men.

Mad Dog raced through gravel, uncertain how to find the exit. A moment later, he identified it by the bright, flashing lights on police cars streaming toward them. And, with that, a domino cascade began.

* * *

Goo Goo Ellison stood in the St Louis Detention Center waiting room. It had been a particularly wild Friday night. Egan's attorney would arrive soon. He turned when he heard the door. He was surprised to see Tony.

"What are you doing here, Coletta?" he said.

"Same as you. They nabbed one of our boys too," Coletta looked around the empty room. "Now Mr. G thinks the Rock House pieces were taken by the Chicago mob with help from inside. He's at a boilin' point."

"Still? After wipin' out the Cuckoos? And puttin' the pinch on the Russo gang? Mr. G's been on a rampage," Goo Goo said. "Egan's been watchin'. Things have changed here. He's talkin' about movin' back east."

"You goin' with him?" Coletta gave him a sideways glance.

"Do we really have a choice?" Goo Goo lamented.

Three men entered the room from inside the detention center. The one who appeared to be in charge spoke. "Which one of you is Mr. Ellison?"

Goo Goo motioned with his hand.

"And you are?" the man said, looking at Coletta.

"Anthony…"

"Coletta," the man cut in. "You guys are wasting your time. Your buddies were busted for multiple offenses on Federal property. They're not going anywhere." He handed each of them his card, on which they saw the FBI's emblem.

After the three men left, Coletta said, "What's with this? The FBI's pokin' around?"

"First I heard of it. And what's he mean about Federal property?" Goo Goo's eyes narrowed.

"Must be because the Arch is a federal project. The whole eighty acres is owned by the feds." Tony Coletta's shoulders slumped.

Goo Goo looked at the FBI card. "We should talk. I think we got a choice to make after all."

* * *

A few days later, five men sat around a table in the St Louis FBI office.

"Both Coletta and Ellison came forward. Their testimonies along with our investigations should close the book on the Egan and Garganelli gangs. We're waiting for the right moment."

A visiting FBI Deputy Director from Washington D.C. said, "Kennedy has been asking if this whole project, the Arch monument, should be scrapped."

"Except for some ongoing union issues, mostly related to discrimination, things will be cleared up soon," another man answered.

"Does the community realize there are an unknown number of murder victims in the base of the north leg?" the Deputy Director asked.

"No. There are only rumors and jokes."

"And you've never located the rest of the Rock House? The President is asking. It was the oldest standing building in St. Louis. JFK holds historical buildings in high esteem."

"We have not. Much of the building is in storage. The rest has disappeared."

"That's a shame. I don't think it will kill the Arch though. It's too far along." The Deputy Director smiled. "Unless there's excessive talk about cement riddled with skeletal remains. We shouldn't include anything about that in the charges or trials. It never happened."

The men nodded in solemn agreement.

Graverobber Blues
C.A. Fehmel

Brenda adjusted her glasses and gazed at the St. Louis Arch reflecting the sun off its stainless-steel façade. That wasn't why she was near the Mississippi riverfront, but it was still impressive. She turned to face the life-sized statue of Harriet and Dred Scott. It was a good likeness based on the few photos that still existed. Most people didn't know Dred Scott lost his initial case on a technicality. It took eleven years of appeals before it reached the Supreme Court.

"What's the point of a speedy trial if justice is so long in coming?" she muttered to herself. Brenda checked her watch again and scanned the parking area. Early on a Saturday, there were still plenty of spaces, which wouldn't be the case in a few hours. Meanwhile, she leaned against her twenty-six-year-old Camry and waited for the Uber driver she'd hired for the day. He was already ten minutes late.

A Prius slowly tooled around the parking lot and pulled to a stop where she stood in front of the statue.

"You Ms. Maxwell?" The young man leaned his head out of the driver's side window.

She whipped out her cell phone to verify his likeness on the Uber website. "I am, and you're late, Brian."

He smiled. Brian had good teeth. "You looked just like my granny when you said that."

"I hope you don't keep her waiting."

"Hop in, let's get going. You texted you had multiple stops."

Brenda tried to tease a smile from her scowl. She was generally easy-going, but one of her pet peeves was people who made you wait and then rushed you as if their lateness was your fault. "Since you're here, you should at least put your car in park and look at this statue of the Scotts."

Brian made a show of looking the statue up-and-down twice, still leaning out of the car window. "Nice." He tipped his head toward the backseat.

Brenda's scowl returned. This was a young man who needed some schooling in manners as well as their culture. It's just as well she'd chosen him to do the driving on her historical sites tour.

"Do you know who Dred Scott was?" She opened the rear door and was glad to see the upholstery was clean. The air-freshener had a subtle pine scent.

"Umm, something to do with slavery. Don't you know?"

Brenda scoffed, "Yeah, I know he filed suit he ought to be free since his slave owner brought him to a free state. He lost, then it was retried. He won, but it was appealed. He lost again."

"He lost?" Brian shook his head. "Not sure we should celebrate that."

"The verdicts kept being appealed. It went all the way to the Supreme Court. Historians say it was so divisive at the time, his case probably precipitated the Civil War."

Brenda couldn't be sure but thought Brian might've suppressed a sigh. "Where to first?"

She tossed a sheet of paper into the front seat.

Brian took a look. The typed flyer was titled "Search St. Louis" sponsored by the local library system. It featured a list of places and addresses, some with thumbnail photos alongside.

"I've highlighted the ones we're going to see." Brenda watched as Brian perused the sheet. He started to type the first address into his phone, set on the holder fastened to his dashboard. "That first one is on the east side of the civil courts building just up a few blocks. No need to get directions."

"I'm not so sure you need an Uber to get to it either," Brian murmured low enough, she almost didn't hear.

Brenda figured she'd get some push-back with the multiple stops, but she was sure this kid needed to learn about their Black culture as much as she wanted to see the places herself. The Prius turned corners, to bypass the one-way streets. Brenda liked that Brian used his turn signals and seemed to be a responsible driver.

"There, right ahead," Brenda said. Once again, the early morning downtown provided a parallel parking spot that would be wishful thinking later. "C'mon."

Brian didn't bother to suppress a sigh this time. He hoped for a big tip from this multi-stop fare, but he hadn't thought he'd have to get out and stand around every time they reached a destination.

Brenda used her phone to take photos. The Freedom Suits Memorial was a dark bronze sculpture, about fourteen feet high, and an unusual shape. From a distance it looked like an off-kilter city scape, but up close it had a lot of faces and information carved into it. The base was a rectangle with a series of names.

"What's this now?" Brian asked, as his curiosity got the better of him. He'd driven past and never really noticed the memorial before. "Is this like a former battle ground? Are these people dead?"

"They're dead," Brenda nodded, "But not from that kind of battle. These were all slaves who filed suit against their owners for their freedom."

"No kidding? Sweet. Did they win?"

Brenda peered at him over her glasses. "Only about a third."

She pressed the photo icon on her phone and got a picture of Brian in front of the memorial. "But they still tried. We honor them as the first freedom fighters."

"At least the cases didn't get yeeted," Brian said.

"What?"

Brian smirked. He enjoyed turning the tables on his ersatz history instructor. "Yeet, as in to toss or to throw. It's a historical term."

Brenda looked skeptical and brandished her phone again. "How do you spell that?"

"Y-e-e-t." He hoped that was right. He'd never written it down, and in truth hadn't used it before.

Brenda found it on her phone. "It's slang from the aughts. That's not historical. I don't even know if slang is considered a real word."

"It's historical if it was invented when you were only three years old."

Brenda shook her head, but he heard her giggle all the same.

They made their way to the Annie Malone House. They speculated why everybody knew Madame C.J. Walker was a famous cosmetics entrepreneur, but few St. Louisans knew anything about Annie Malone. She was entrepreneurial too, and a philanthropist who donated the building as a home for orphaned children.

Brian invited Brenda to sit up front when they left the Annie Malone House. He said it was so she could help him navigate, but the closeness allowed their discussions to grow more involved. They visited Tandy Park, where he'd spent some good times on the playground, unaware Tandy was an educator and civil rights activist.

"Where to next?" Brian said, now fully invested in their search.

"Quinette, it's the oldest African American cemetery west of the Mississippi."

"A cemetery?" Brian considered. "Are there any famous Black actors buried there?"

Brenda scanned the flyer. "It doesn't say, but they'd be older actors from Hollywood's golden age, not seventies action stars like Ron O'Neal from 'Superfly'."

"Don't be judgy. My granny loves movies, and we've watched all the classics with Dorothy Dandridge and Lena Horne."

Brian pulled onto the highway now that they were leaving St. Louis city and heading west into the county.

"I'm impressed. Do you know who Hattie McDaniel was?"

"Mammy from 'Gone with the Wind.' And don't forget Butterly McQueen as Prissy. She stole every scene she was in."

Brenda giggled. "Well, I was talking to my girlfriend, Donna, before one of the Black History Month concerts. She'd checked out a library book about Hattie McDaniel called 'The Queen of Sugar Hill.' Donna said she was fascinated because her great, great uncle had gone to Howard University. He used to get a sly smile on his face whenever he talked about Hattie McDaniel's Oscar."

"That Oscar was stolen, right? Granny told me that."

Brenda nodded. She warmed to the intrigue. "It went missing. It was part of Donna's family lore that it's buried with her Uncle David out at Quinette."

"No. For real?"

"Nobody knows. They never found the Oscar. Donna said it's been a minute since she's been out there. She meant to go visit Uncle David's grave, but Quinette is hard to find. Then she griped because all the places on this flyer were historical. She thought there should be modern landmarks on there too."

"Can something be modern and still a landmark?"

"Yeah, but really she just wanted Heru's Urban Farm to be included because Heru is one fine looking man."

Brian grinned. "You interested? Is that jealousy I hear?"

Brenda giggled again. "If I was going to choose a man based on his occupation, I'd be interested in a mechanic, not a farmer."

"You sure? Because you mentioned the farmer was good looking right up front."

"I'm sure." Brenda's smile widened. "I wasn't the only one interested. There was some nosy guy who kept asking Donna questions. We had to change seats once the concert started so he'd leave us alone."

"Maybe he was interested in you," Brian teased.

"Well, it was a concert, and I was interested in jazz."

The map on his phone indicated they were close. They were both frustrated Quinette wasn't well-marked. Brenda read from the flyer the graveyard had been wrested from the hands of developers who envisioned condos and mixed retail space.

"I hope somebody yeeted those development plans right back in their faces," Brenda said testing her new vocabulary word. She liked the feel of it.

"I think that's it," Brian said as they passed the same small, wooded area for the sixth time.

Brian pulled into a nearby parking lot. They got out and trudged up a small incline toward the wooded area. He steadied her over the rough spots. He'd been taught good manners and respect. Now he could add knowledge of Black history to that list.

They found the wrought iron gate entrance. Inside it was nice and shady, the mature trees standing sentinel with branches spread like protective hands over worn tombstones. The walking paths were narrow and meandered through the trees. A few tombstones had fallen over, and many were so worn, the names and dates were just faint imprints. Brenda had brought paper and a charcoal stick, determined to take a rubbing to remember her trip today. She'd just started to kneel near one where she could at least make out the name and date, when she heard a rhythmic series of crunches in the distant part of the grove.

Brenda strained to see over the dense brush and wooded area. Brenda pulled back and grabbed Brian's arm. He dug in his heels, but she pulled harder, jerking her head to the side to indicate a large tree.

"What—" but Brian didn't get a chance to finish his sentence.

Brenda gave him the universal 'shush' signal known to librarians everywhere.

They stood, backs against the black walnut tree and pressed against it hard enough to feel the rough bark.

Brian leaned down to whisper in Brenda's ear. "What's going on? I thought you said this was a public park even though it's like, impossible to find."

"It is public, but they're not using it to bury people anymore. Somebody is back there digging a grave."

Brian snorted. "What? No. There's a funeral going on?"

"Not a legal one!"

"Nobody buries a body in broad daylight unless it's a funeral."

"Then you tell me what they're doing. That's not like any funeral I've ever seen."

Brian was a good deal taller than Brenda. He padded along the mulch trail, which was damp and therefore rather quiet. Peering beyond the brush, he saw a man who looked as if he'd been cut off at the knees, but it was only because he'd dug pretty far down already. Brian was mesmerized. Mounds of dirt were on either side of the grave. The unknown man tossed, or maybe he should say, yeeted, more clumps of dirt from the hole to the side. A gravestone sat askew at the head of the hole. Brian's eyes widened. "Yikes."

Brian darted back to the walnut tree where the fear in Brenda's eyes mirrored his own. "You're right, but I don't think he's burying a body. He's digging one up."

"What?!" Brenda asked. She was so nervous, her voice squeaked.

"Keep your voice down. We spent most of the morning seeing people try to use the law to get justice, and from what you said, it rarely happens."

Brenda's eyes narrowed. "Did you get a look at the guy?"

"Yeah, so? I'm not going to testify. I'm not going near a courtroom."

"I've watched enough Law & Order episodes to know he's not legally exhuming a body back there."

Brian shook his head and continued to keep his voice low. 'How do you know? Maybe it's some historian or an archeological dig."

"If it was an archeological dig, there'd be a news crew and a brass band." Brenda was disgusted, she also had a hunch. She crept forward, hid behind the mature trees, since the gravestones were too small to give much cover. The invasive bush honeysuckle made itself useful. Its green foliage was dense enough to give her cover, but she could see clear through to the other side. The graverobber paused, wiped his brow despite it being rather chilly and windy. The grave was deeper than she would've supposed.

As he lowered his hand, Brenda confirmed what she feared. Brian joined Brenda, hunched down, and peeked through the foliage.

She elbowed him in the gut. "That's the nosy guy!"

"What? Are you sure?"

Brenda was angry, angry at the disrespect of digging someone up, and based on an offhand comment she was privy to. She tugged her phone out of her pocket.

Brian shook his head. "What are you doing?"

"Calling 9-1-1. He's committing a crime as well as disrespecting the dead." Her whisper contained venom.

He shook his head harder. "Do not call the cops to come out here with us the only witnesses."

"Why not?"

"Because he has a shovel, and we have…our phones."

Brenda nodded. "Let's yeet caution to the wind. You go call the cops. I'm going to videotape this jerk."

Brian shook his head again. "You call the cops. I'll videotape."

They both put their phones against the wall of bush honeysuckle and started to record. The gravedigger didn't hear their quiet exchange because he was making a racket of his own. In addition to the shovel, he had a crowbar. He traded one tool for the other and disappeared into the hole. The old wood being torn asunder shrieked and groaned as if it protested the loss of its treasures.

"It has got to be in here." The graverobber stood. Only his head and shoulders showed above the mounded soil. He bent and disappeared from view.

Brenda heard a sharp crack, like a dry branch breaking. A skeletal arm flew from the coffin.

"Oh no you don't!" Brenda shouted. Her phone still out in front of her, she rounded the honeysuckle and stomped through the clods of mud to where the man stood over the open coffin.

Brian tried to pull her back, but to no avail. "Brenda!"

The graverobber turned. The newly exhumed skeleton smiled with dirty teeth.

"Cease and desist! This is a citizen's arrest!" Brenda said.

The graverobber stood on the lower part of the coffin, having ripped open the top half. He leapt with surprising agility up the disheveled earth at the end of the grave, and landed right in front of Brenda, the crowbar still in his hand. "Oh, yeah, who's gonna stop me?"

Brenda tried to speak, but only a squeak came out. He knocked the phone out of her hand and watched it bounce into the open grave. A sudden thrust of the crowbar near her face caused her head to snap back.

"You need to go back to your car, mind your own business." He gave her a push. "You were never here and didn't see anything."

Brenda started to tremble so hard the graverobber could see her shake.

"Go on now," he coaxed. "I see you're scared."

Brenda lunged forward, felt the hard iron of the crowbar against her face as she shoved the thief as hard as she could. He stumbled, lost his footing, and fell backward into the grave. The remaining arm of the skeleton broke at the elbow and raised against the flailing arm of the newcomer. To Brenda it looked like the dead man saluted her.

"That wasn't fear. That was anger." She bent down and lifted the shovel. "You just stay right there, mister."

The skeleton seemed to smile more widely now.

"Brenda! Brenda you were amazing!" Brian came up behind her.

"Where were you?" Brenda asked, though her eyes remained on the scene in the grave.

"I called the police. I shouldn't have to tell you how foolish it was to confront this guy."

"It was the right thing to do," Brenda said in her defense. Approaching sirens punctuated her statement.

The cops made quick work of apprehending the graverobber and taking statements. Brenda had called her friend Donna, and suggested they be there when her Uncle David's new coffin was re-buried in Quinette. She had to call Donna on Brian's phone, however, because the police had fished hers from within the ribcage of the skeleton, and then confiscated it for evidence.

By now it was dusk, but not yet dark. The flashing lights of the police cars pulled away. Brenda and Brian picked their way along one of the wood chip paths around the gravestones.

"Well, this definitely made an impression on me, if that was your goal," Brian said as they reached the road.

"I didn't intend for there to be this much action," Brenda said. "But I am glad you were here with me."

"My pleasure, my pleasure. Too bad we didn't get to all the places you marked on your list."

"What are you doing tomorrow? It's Sunday, but you don't look like the church going type."

"Seriously? You're still up for it?"

"If today has proven anything it's that we have a long history of people who fight to do the right thing. I'm not going to throw in the towel now."

Brian smiled. He had good teeth. "You mean yeet in the towel, don't you? Brenda, I think this is the beginning of a beautiful friendship."

Tell No Lies
Stormy White

I've never thought honesty is the best policy.

Let me illustrate. An individual in my profession recklessly answered honestly when asked what he did for a living. There was no fascination or admiration as depicted in movies and novels. He was shunned and lived an isolated existence until a former employer became alarmed and instigated a termination.

His honesty was a mistake.

I do not make mistakes. Nor am I reckless. In fact, last year only one of my targets was even recognized as a premeditated killing.

I am the crème de la crème, best of the best, in a society in which money rules and everything is for sale.

Still, I feel bad about the doctor. By all accounts, he was a good person. Though, I did enjoy my visit to St. Louis and expect to return.

* * *

Twenty-year-old Nora Atherton glanced around the empty office and asked, "How could they lose all applications?"

A woman wearing eight-hundred-dollar Louboutin shoes answered, "Shredding and deleting. Because of the lawsuit. My husband's their lawyer and he's furious. That is a big no-no. Everybody's yelling."

The woman sensed Nora's desperation. "I am sorry. Where did you go to high school?"

It was a simple question.

But this was St. Louis, and the question really was how rich is your family, are you Catholic? How smart are you? It had taken her a month to figure that out.

Could this woman get her a job if she gave the right answer? Her application was destroyed.

Why not lie?

Because she had vowed no more lies.

She answered, "My parents sent me to school in New Hampshire."

It wasn't really a lie. Her parents indirectly sent her to school in New Hampshire by letting her Aunt Agnes take custody when they were sent to prison after being convicted of embezzlement in Washington, D.C.

"New Hampshire? Oh, Exeter Academy." The woman grabbed a slip of paper and began writing an address. "Excellent. This is perfect. My friend's husband desperately needs a clerk. Gloria will be so pleased. I'll call Dr. Ripon's office to tell them you're on your way."

Nora cringed. Wasn't Exeter Academy a boarding school for rich kids? Her "not really a lie" had turned into a super lie.

The transition from the diverse environment of Washington, D.C. to the small town of Hanover, New Hampshire, was difficult. There was the additional burden that to avoid the embarrassment of people knowing she had relatives convicted of felonies, Aunt Agnes told everyone Nora's parents were missionaries kidnapped by terrorists in the Congo.

The college where Agnes worked had worldwide connections. The web of lies to maintain the secret became so complicated all Nora could do was look sad and keep her mouth shut. The high school was excellent, but it had been the most excruciating four years of her life.

She left immediately after graduation for California. After three years of odd jobs and earning an associate degree in Fine Arts from the College of San Mateo, she was now in St Louis with her parents. They had flat timed their sentences, so there was no parole.

It was awkward.

Her parents said nothing about those years except, "No expert could say the coins were forgeries, only that they did not appear to be the coins offered by the seller."

The other would agree, "That's why they couldn't prove forgery. But we shouldn't have …"

"I agree."

It was always on the tip of Nora's tongue to ask, "Forgery or embezzlement, does it matter?" Better to forget those years and not ask how they acquired a house in St. Louis.

The house was a beautifully restored two-story, four-bedroom, red brick home with a terracotta tiled roof near the Missouri Botanical Gardens, a lovely neighborhood regaining its former prestige.

Her parents were soul mates and their time apart, not knowing how the other was faring, had left scars. For seven years, Nora told herself, life would be the way it was when they were together again.

But it wasn't the way it was.

They were different and so was she. She could tell by the lines in their faces their pain was equal to hers.

It was time to move on and the first step was to stop lying.

St. Louis was a perfect choice, large but not too large, fantastic museums and attractions, even the humid July heat wasn't keeping them from making new memories.

Nora's favorite place was the St. Louis Zoo, her mother's favorite was the flood wall at the Mississippi River with its colorful graffiti, and her father's favorite was the graffiti in a vibrant neighborhood called The Grove.

But Nora's savings were gone, and she couldn't shake the fear her parents might return to crime. She was desperate for an income.

The job the woman mentioned was working for Dr. Ripon who treated patients with bladder issues. She interviewed at his office close to Forest Park.

Dr. Walter Ripon looked like a movie star. He was tall, dark hair graying at the temples, piercing blue eyes, and had perfectly symmetrical features characteristic of handsome humans. "So, you have a degree in art?"

"An associate degree."

"No desire to become a scientist, a medical researcher?"

Yes was probably the right answer, but the honest answer was no. Nora felt herself blush. "Sorry, Sir, not really."

Walter Ripon smiled. "We can't go wrong with an Exeter graduate. Welcome. Cora will show you what to do. Of course, we want an NDA."

Aunt Agnes lectures were always popping into her mind. They always began, "Your parents aren't here, so it's my duty to instruct you."

Today, she remembered, "Beware of people super good-looking, super rich, or super smart. Their super attribute normally leaves them deficient in some area."

She pushed the thought away. Why a nondisclosure agreement? What did it matter? It was a good paying job.

Cora, a no-nonsense woman in nurse's scrubs, entered with papers for her to sign. She explained the duties were not to socialize, not to gossip, merely enter data into the computer, print the forms, file the printouts, and on certain days, fill in for Mrs. Ripon's personal assistant. She closed with, "I'm assigning you Dr. David Marks' parking space."

* * *

The job was lonely and boring but easy.

At noon, on Friday of the fourth week, Cora told her to go to the Ripon home for an orientation because she was working there the following week.

She was amazed to discover a three-story, gray stone mansion in an exclusive neighborhood off Clayton Road. Given the traditional French architecture of the exterior, the shimmering modern metal sculptures in the entrance hall were a surprise.

The grandeur of the estate brought to mind another Aunt Agnes lecture, "Know the source of the money and assume nothing."

Gloria Ripon greeted her in the entrance hall as if they were old friends, introduced Anne, her personal assistant, and excused herself.

Gloria was another movie-star human, a perfect match for Dr. Ripon.

Gloria's personal assistant reminded Nora of the girls in high school she would have liked to have had as friends but avoided because she might let something slip and embarrass her aunt. Anne had disheveled, short blond hair and was wearing a wrinkled Navy-blue linen dress with a jade pendant and white sneakers. Her smile was quick and genuine.

In a room off the library, she held up a notebook. "I've copied my notes for you. I never remember who is who. Probably because I don't give a damn Jackie what's-her-name got invited to the Met Gala. Whoops. Wrong notebook."

Her eyes teared. "That belonged to David. I wanted to keep something of his."

She carefully replaced it on her desk.

"Who is David?"

Anne's eyes welled again. "Dr. David Marks, a brilliant man who cared about people. He was mugged outside his condo."

That was unnerving. "I'm sorry." She hesitated and asked, "Do I babysit?"

"Oh no. Gertie, the nanny, takes care of the kids. Sometimes Benny helps because he adores them. The personal assistant coordinates appointments with events. For example, Gloria is going to a dinner dance tonight where there will be photos, so I had to make sure she had hair and manicure appointments this morning and her make-up lady is coming at five. Her clothes are ready and I made sure she hadn't previously been photographed wearing them."

Nora's face must have shown her shock because Anne laughed. "I know. Don't worry. There's nothing next week except a luncheon. I've already laid out her clothes for the meeting with the Exeter Academy graduate. She also wants some boxes moved."

Nora's heart beat faster. Was this irony? After all the lies she'd participated in, she was going to be caught in one she never intended.

Anne continued, "Benny will help. The important thing to remember is Gloria wants to look perfect in every way on every day."

She paused. "I should write that phrase down. Gloria has fund raisers, invites people, they donate, and she gets the credit. I tried to convince her to do an event to save the pangolins, but she laughed, saying what does that get me? A thank you from the weirdos of the world?"

Nora knew about pangolins because during her isolated high school years she watched every documentary on PBS. Trying to save pangolins seemed admirable.

Anne said, "The Exeter guy coming Monday seems charming. Very inquisitive though."

Panic in her voice, Anne asked, "You aren't thinking of bailing, are you? Gloria would insist I stay and next week I'm volunteering in Costa Rico to help save the leatherback sea turtles."

Anne whispered, "The truth is I hate this job. I only got hired because they have a thing about private schools, and I graduated from John Burroughs High School." She added, "And she thought my mom had been a Veiled Prophet Queen."

Another Aunt Agnes Rule flashed into Nora's head, "Know the people in power, their past and present." What was a Veiled Prophet Queen?

Anne continued, "I only stayed here so I could see David and now he's gone…"

Anne suddenly raised her voice, "So you can see why I'm worried."

Nora turned to see Gloria had joined them.

Anne announced, "I was explaining why I'm so worried about Ruby and Forest."

Gloria looked confused and then frowned, "Oh, those zoo orangutans."

Nora said, "She was telling me how grateful she is you support the zoo." She thought, damn, that makes Anne look good, but it's a lie.

Determined not to break her vow of no lying, she added, "That's what I heard." She thought, no, that's just a different lie.

Try again. "I love the St. Louis Zoo."

Gloria frowned. "Yes, we all love the zoo. Just wanted to remind Nora the meeting on Monday with Phillip is at the club so dress appropriately. Anne, have a great week in Mexico."

"Costa Rico."

The rest of the afternoon was spent learning a few rules, touring the house, and meeting Maria, the cook-housekeeper, Gertie, the nanny, the twins, and Benny, the driver-handyman. There were back stairs, front stairs, and an elevator that went from the basement to the third floor. Staff were to use the back stairs and only the bathrooms on the third floor. Nora involuntarily uttered, "That sucks."

Anne laughed, "Tell me about it. One minute Gloria acts like you're best friends, the next it's Upstairs Downstairs and you belong downstairs. Be careful, the darling twins love to tattle if they discover you use a bathroom on the first or second floors."

Anne talked nonstop about David Marks, his integrity, intelligence, and gorgeous brown eyes.

"Did I replace an actual doctor?"

"Oh no. David and Walter were friends. Walter got some grant and wanted David's help writing the results. Your job was created by Walter and Cora after David died."

* * *

Nora's parents cooked that day, cream of broccoli soup, a sirloin roast, fresh rolls, roasted potatoes, a garden salad, and chocolate mousse for dessert. After so many years of not being able to cook, when they cooked, they *cooked*.

Nora's stress was astronomical. The money her parents spent on groceries was mind-blowing, their constant questioning as if she were still fourteen was annoying, and her concern they might do something illegal was constant.

Also, they were sneaking out at night and gone for hours. Now she had the worry she would be fired as soon as it was discovered she never attended Exeter. As much as she wanted to hide in her room, she couldn't say no to eating with them. But she didn't have her usual

51

energy to make her day sound pleasant and blurted out every detail.

Suddenly her parents were like different people demanding she sketch the sculptures she'd seen in the Ripon home, asking questions like "Exactly where was this David assaulted? Are you sure four people work full-time in the home?"

Nora went to bed early but not before she overheard them on the computer:

"This Marks incident is disturbing. Doesn't look like a mugging."

"What about an office employee working as a personal assistant for a wife?"

They began to discuss how odd Nora was the only public-school graduate Ripon hired. Even the driver, Benny, was a private school graduate.

Nora felt worse. After advocating 'tell no lies' was the best policy, how could she tell them she let her employers believe a lie?

Wait, how did they know where Benny went to high school?

Monday morning Nora arrived at the Ripon residence prepared for utter humiliation. The first surprise was to see Cora from the office. She handed Nora a set of keys with an admonition the van was to be used only to transport boxes. She asked, "If this Phillip Black asks what common denominator Dr. Ripon's patients have, what do you say?"

Answers raced through Nora's mind, their age, bladder issues, insurance. She realized it was a test. "I'd answer, I'm not at liberty to say."

Cora nodded. "Just checking."

The next hour Gloria showed her closets and storage areas filled with sealed boxes. "I'm re-decorating and making the entrance hall larger. I want these boxes and the ones in the basement moved. Cora's keeping those labelled 'David Marks' so you can put them in the van. Put the others in the garage. Benny will help."

"Where do I drive the van?"

"Cora will explain. Also, change of plans, Phillip wants to meet here. I'm going to change. Ask Maria if she needs help in the kitchen."

Maria was in a foul mood and told Nora to leave because she now had to prepare a fancy lunch as well as lunch for the nanny and kids.

Anticipating the disaster to come, Nora tried to think how she could explain she hadn't attended Exeter. She gave up the idea because the stress of living with lies was too much pressure. She went to Anne's desk and studied the notebooks. Gloria Ripon would never be embarrassed by wearing the wrong thing or seen wearing the same thing twice.

She found newspaper articles describing David Marks' death. He had been shot in the back of the head in the parking lot of his condo. He was thirty-six and described as a prominent urologist.

She thumbed through Marks' notebook. He had names, dates, and exclamation marks. Weird. Many names looked familiar.

The next surprise was Phillip Black. He was muscular, clean shaven, with wire-rimmed glasses, a tweed sports jacket, and Khaki trousers. He was handsome, sexy, personable, and met the criteria of every Aunt Agnes warning. He looked you in the eye when he talked, no excessive blinking, and didn't look to either side when he answered questions.

Phillip Black exhibited the traits of a man well-trained to lie.

Gloria introduced him as an Exeter Academy and Harvard University educated architect whose firm had designed for every famous person you could name.

He shook Nora's hand, held it a second longer than normal, looked her in the eyes and smiled, "Always a pleasure to meet an Exeter alumna."

Phillip and Gloria looked at pictures of entrance halls through lunch of clam chowder and miniature beef Wellingtons followed by chocolate cheesecake. Nora took notes and wondered if Gloria saw through Phillip's manipulations. More than once he commented, "I knew you'd like that idea. Intelligent, artistic people always do."

After lunch they walked through the house. Phillip took photos and measurements with a fancy laser tape measure. Why would he take photos of boxes that had belonged to David Marks?

It was after three o'clock when Phillip was ready to leave. Gloria smiled, "Nora will walk you to your car."

At the white rental car, he handed her a bag. "A necklace designed by an Exeter graduate in my class. It's got the Exeter seal in eighteen-karat gold. Do you ever go to re-unions?"

She said thank you, no reunions. If he would just leave, everything might be okay. No one had questioned her about Exeter, so technically she had told no lies.

Did people go to reunions three years out of high school? Every instinct told her this man shouldn't be trusted.

He asked, "So where did you go to college?"

Aunt Agnes's voice in her mind said, "If possible, give no information. At least be vague. Asking a question always helps." Nora smiled, "California. Is there a copyright issue with the Exeter seal on the necklace?"

He shrugged and drove away.

Relief flooded Nora. Anne would be back, and she might never have to see him again.

Happy to return home and still employed, she was greeted by a smiling neighbor. "You must be so proud of your parents. Imagine how difficult it was to teach computer technology to French speaking African entrepreneurs."

Why would they make up such things? She followed an Aunt Agnes axiom, "Just smile." Was not correcting someone the same as a lie?

Her parents had prepared another dinner, this time duplicating a meal from a health food café, greens and onions, beans and rice, and yucca cakes.

If they were going to duplicate local food, why not barbecue? Pappy's barbecue was the best she'd ever tasted. Or was it Bogart's? She loved all St Louis barbecue. Health food made her appreciate it even more.

Grateful they were more interested in hearing about her day than what she thought of dinner, she was vague in details concerning Phillip Black. They detected her reluctance and persisted in asking questions. To change the subject, she showed them the necklace.

"A necklace celebrating Exeter Academy?" asked her mother.

Too late Nora realized they would wonder why such a gift. Her mother's expression became her poker face, and she handed the necklace to her husband. "Rob, take a look."

His face was impossible to read. "Let's go."

Nora watched her parents leave with the necklace. Confused, worried, and a little afraid, she waited. When they returned, her father apologized, "Sorry. It's better whoever gave you that necklace isn't positive where you live."

Her mother explained, "It contained a tracker. We left it at an apartment on Lindell."

"A tracker? Are you sure?"

That was crazy. Maybe her parents were wrong. She claimed she had a headache and went to bed.

The next morning, after barely any sleep, she left without talking to them. How did they know about trackers? Why weren't they worried about money? Where did they go at night? She hoped it was to paint graffiti, or maybe they'd found a jazz bar they liked. St. Louis had great jazz bars.

"Always know the source of the money and assume nothing" kept running through her mind, plus another Aunt Agnes directive, "Never ignore a fact because it makes you uncomfortable."

The Ripon lifestyle was expensive. They had a mansion, two cars, a nanny, a driver-handyman, housekeeper-cook, and personal assistant. Doctors made good money, but enough money for all that? It could be inherited money, maybe lottery money. Why hadn't she asked Aunt Agnes how to discover these things?

Thinking of money reminded Nora as the only wage-earning member of the household, she couldn't afford to displease her employers. Time to find Benny and move boxes.

When she found him, Nora didn't scream or cry. She stood stunned and then ran to the house.

Within minutes, the police, an ambulance, and a firetruck arrived.

Benny's body was in front of the garage, his blood and brains splattered on the brick driveway.

It appeared Benny had placed the barrel of a .40 caliber Smith & Wesson pistol in his mouth and pulled the trigger. No one heard or if they did, it hadn't registered as a gunshot. A man in a suit questioned Nora about any strangers on the property. He looked miffed by her answers.

She felt numb. Would Benny kill himself in a place where the kids could see? No one asked her opinion. She didn't offer it.

The police asked about a suicide note and walked through the house. Nora saw someone pick up the notebooks on Anne's desk and objected. "Those aren't Benny's. I'll take them."

Dr. Ripon returned home with Cora. She heard, "Phone call for Nora."

She answered the extension in the kitchen, "Yes?"

A voice growled "Why are David Marks boxes still in existence?"

She stuttered, "In existence? I was going to move them and found Benny."

"Cora?"

Nora knew this was a time to lie but not a person to lie to. She choked, "Cora or Nora?"

The line went dead.

"Was that for me?" asked Cora.

Nora tried to think of an Aunt Agnes lecture but couldn't. She pretended not to hear and asked how long Benny had worked for the Ripon family.

"Twelve years." The look in Cora's eyes said she knew the call was for her and Nora should *not* have taken it.

Gloria appeared and announced, "This is too chaotic. I'm taking Gertie and the children to the cottage." She looked at Nora, "Maria's driving us, so I won't need you. Concentrate on those closets."

Nora didn't know whether she was more shocked at Gloria's lack of emotion at Benny's death or that she thought she could demand Nora travel out of town.

Cora watched her. "They have a house on Lake Michigan. Go home. The police should be gone by six. Come back then. A key to the kitchen door is on the key ring with the van keys. We'll leave the alarm system off."

* * *

Nora was too drained to object when her parents took the notebooks. Intending to take a short nap, she fell into a deep sleep. It was six-thirty when she woke. She immediately left.

It was almost seven when she reached the mansion. It was spooky to be alone in the enormous home. She heard noises everywhere, clocks ticked, a computer dinged, and appliances hummed.

There was a message from Gloria for her to send flowers to Benny's funeral with a card from the family. Walter was flying to the cottage and would be there for a week. She added Nora could attend Benny's funeral but otherwise keep clearing boxes. Cora would give her further instructions.

This was not such a good job. She hadn't seen a single tear for Benny.

She pulled boxes from the closets in the front hall. Geesh, why so many and why were they here? Curious, she opened a box. It was filled with personal mail, note pads, flash drives, phones, and laptop computer. Someone had scooped David Marks' belongings into a box. Another box had copies of autopsies.

How many of David's boxes were in the basement?

She took the elevator to the basement. In the dim light, she counted a dozen boxes already stacked nearby. She walked to the stairs and stifled a scream. Cora lay at the bottom of the steps with a leg twisted under her. No pulse.

Nora started to dial 911 but turned when she sensed movement behind her. Phillip Black walked towards her.

There was no one to hear. She screamed anyway.

Someone called her name from the top of the stairs.

"Mom, Dad?"

"There you are." Her parents, followed by two men, came downstairs, careful to step over Cora.

A figure came from the shadows. "Aunt Agnes!" gasped Nora. "How…"

"Your parents called. I'll explain later. *Please*, stop screaming."

* * *

Phillip Black and his men weren't taking any chances boxes had been mislabeled. The entire house was searched. All boxes were carried out and loaded into a truck.

Nora stood in the driveway with her parents and Aunt Agnes. "Should we do something? Maybe ask for a receipt?"

She caught the look from her parents and remembered an Aunt Agnes lecture. "There will be times when not only do you want to practice 'silence is golden', but people must also know you practice it."

Before Phillip Black got in the truck, he gave Agnes a hug, shook hands with Nora's parents, and whispered to Nora, "I'd get another job."

When he was gone, Nora choked, "Did Phillip, I mean did someone, I mean is Cora's death an accident?"

Agnes sighed, "No, dear. Not given the amount of money she and Dr. Ripon put at risk. But not Phillip. Phillip is ex-government and freelances but he's no killer."

Agnes took Nora aside. "Your parents are talented forgers, manipulated into a scheme not of their doing. They stayed silent, but their forgery days are over. They are resourceful, and you shouldn't worry. I've told them you're no longer a child, they should talk with you. I applaud your vow to tell no lies. For some of us, there is a difference between lying and telling a story."

She gave her a hug. "Get on with your life. Enjoy St. Louis. Do you know how many colleges and universities are here? Sports events?"

Agnes walked away grinning, "Last lecture. What's legal may not be right and what's illegal may not be wrong. Think about it, it used to be illegal to teach folks of color to read and write."

The police responded to Nora's 911 call and were gone in less than an hour. They were convinced Cora slipped on the stairs and hit her head.

* * *

Nora sat in the living room as her father began, "First, never think prison isn't horrible. It destroys some people. We were lucky, met a few good people, helped some people, and learned new skills."

Her mother added, "We survived by concentrating on the positive. We were fortunate we had Agnes to care for you. We taught skills to grateful people. Learned how to access information and earned favors which allowed us to acquire a house anywhere we wanted."

The skills acquired by her parents let them unravel what happened.

Her father explained, "For years, Walter Ripon and Cora billed insurance companies for procedures not performed, patients never treated. Eager for more money, they thought a grant would be just the thing. More money and prestige. They asked David Marks to help report their data."

Nora's mother shook her head. "It never occurred to them David's allegiance would be with patients."

"Marks discovered their scheme and was appalled. Most upsetting, they denied patients treatments to get the results they wanted. He was determined to stop them," her father added.

"Unfortunately, Marks never suspected Ripon and Cora were connected to an organization that collected billions from insurance companies that paid pharmacies, laboratories, and facilities that didn't exist. When so much money is involved, so are serious people. Those people were alerted when Marks notified authorities." Her mother sighed. "He was eliminated. Ripon and Cora were instructed to destroy Marks' evidence and create paperwork to back up their billing. With Marks dead, his proof gone, the authorities tried to persuade Benny to cooperate. He doomed himself the minute he agreed."

"Cora told them Marks' proof was destroyed. They wanted to be sure and sent Phillip. He reported Cora lied. Why would she lie?" Nora was in shock at the turn of events.

Her father nodded. "Exactly what they asked. It couldn't be tolerated."

They sat in silence. Nora wanted to ask her parents what they did when they went out at night but decided the easiest way to have no lies was to ask no questions.

Instead, she asked, "You said you could have a house anywhere, why St. Louis?"

Without hesitation they answered, "The Arch. How many places do you think can be identified immediately from the air? The Gateway Arch next to the Mississippi river is unmistakable. A plane can fly over with no radio, blackest night, and know right where they are."

Nora repeated to herself, "Ask no questions and there will be no lies."

The Murder of Saint Archie
(a Madison Silva detective story)
Saralynn Lester

Saint Louis is famous for one single question. No, it's not "Does the Arch straddle the Mississippi?" (It doesn't. We're the Gateway to the WEST, not the Long Float Trip SOUTH to New Orleans.) And it's not "What's up with all the saints?" either. (Even though we have a lot of Saint Everythings around here.)

Saint Louis's favorite question is, "Where'd you go to high school?" Your answer to this critical question explains everything about you. For the rest of your life. When someone asks a new person The Question, everyone freezes, conversation stops, and cats pause in the midst of coughing up hairballs. Then the new person says they're actually from Kansas City. Everyone laughs and goes back to what they were doing. Somewhere Else is uninteresting. Somewhere Else doesn't tell you anything about a person, except they're Other.

I'm not Other. I'm Saint Louis all the way. I live in Kirkwood, which is the best suburb. Everyone wants to live here, no one moves away, and the public schools are better than private. Go, Pioneers! But after a disastrous freshman year at Kirkwood High—bullying, vaping, framing, long story not worth the time—my parents decided to pull me out of public school and send me to Saint Gertrude's. Who even *is* Saint Gertrude? The patron saint of cats, apparently, which I don't care about as I'm allergic.

Anyway, it's a "good school" and will "serve me well for the rest of my life" and "prepare me for my bright future," and who cares that I have to wear a plaid skirt, live in a dorm, and give up my dream of leading the Pioneer Marching Band at the Turkey Day football game against Webster Groves?

Now I'm a Saint Gertrude's Ginger Cat (seriously) and we don't even have a marching band. Rah rah. I guess I'll impress college admissions committees with my resiliency in the face of adversity (forced into boarding school) instead of my future drum-major skills. Maybe I sound dramatic, but just because you're paranoid doesn't mean they're not out to get you.

At my old school, I made a bit of a name for myself as a detective. Not like Nancy Drew, more like Pippa Fitz-Amobi (if you know, you know—A Good Girl's Guide to Murder fans represent). And like Pippa, I made a few enemies along the way. See above re: bullying, vaping, framing, etc. Anyway, my detective reputation followed me to Saint Gertrude's.

My cousin knows a girl named Alyssa at Saint Gertrude's. She's in my year and actually from Kirkwood, so we became friends pretty quickly. Thankfully. The only thing worse than being stuck in a private Catholic boarding school—when I'm not even Catholic—is being stuck in a private Catholic boarding school with no friends. Alyssa and I know people in common, so we were practically already friends before I even met her. She loves to be the center of attention, which means there are always lots of girls around. I've gotten to know people super-fast, especially for a new kid. Alyssa's friends with everyone in our dorm plus everyone in sophomore year plus some of the older students who tutor her (do her work for her) in math and writing and stuff.

I've always been a person who loves a puzzle. Everyone who's ever met me knows it's not just because games are fun. Any mystery gets under my skin like cat dander. Puzzles make me itch until I can slide all the pieces into place. That's probably why my new dormmates come to me for help with everything from a missing hairbrush (Kyly's lonely younger sister took it home with her after a weekend visit) to the source of the roach infestation in Eads Dorm (a first-former, who never learned to clean, hoarded candy and attempted to set up a black-market trading operation—bold for a thirteen-year-old.). Boarding-school kids love drama. I should have anticipated the arrival of my next case as winter turned to false spring.

Missouri is finally starting to come back to life. The days grow longer, we see the sun glint off the Arch in the distance from time to time, and there's a haze of green across the quad. Today I learned my new BFF Alyssa is being blackmailed. It's a pretty ugly situation.

Her family has money—most people at this school do, which is how come all the dorm rooms are singles. Every time Alyssa pays the mysterious jerk who's blackmailing her, they ask for something bigger, more, harder to get. Now, they've asked for the impossible. She has to steal the answer key to the next algebra exam or the blackmailer will kill her secret pet cat, Saint Archie.

Everyone is freaking out for her and we can't tell our dorm mom or resident counselor. We're not allowed to have pets in the dorms, but Alyssa's got a soft spot for stray felines, and I've got a soft spot for Alyssa, so here we are. Or, rather, here I am, playing detective again and sneaking around the darkened dorm after curfew to find out who's sliding these terrifying notes under Alyssa's door.

They're all typewritten—in Comic Sans as an extra crime. And in Haiku form to add insult to injury.

> Post the grading key
> in the Eads lounge by Monday ...
> or Saint Archie dies.

It's not even good poetry.

> How many lives does
> Saint Archie have left, and will
> He survive the week?

Whoever this blackmailer is, they must not have taken Dr. León's sophomore poetry unit yet. Or they should take it again.

Monday. Eads lounge. Noon.
Desprate times, desprate crimes.
I need math answers.

That last one is all kinds of wrong. Spelling, syllables, mess.

I crouched in the third floor's empty bathroom, lights off, door cracked, to watch Alyssa's door. All night. For the seventh night in a row. And for the seventh night in a row, no one comes. The hallway is empty, silent, lit by red exit signs and the occasionally strobing light from a riverboat casino.

Somewhere close, on the darkened floor, a printer whirrs to life.

Her dorm room opens. Alyssa bursts into the hallway and screams, "I got another note!"

And I found the "blackmailer."

Long live Saint Archie.

Achoo.

All. The. Stupid. Genes.
Catina Williams

One question has troubled philosophers since the time of the ancient Greeks. Which dictated human development, nature or nurture? I discovered the answer. Nature. Definitely nature.

Our youngest brother inherited all the stupid genes. My parents worked hard to provide their four children with a stable upbringing. They gave us everything we'd need to develop into upstanding citizens: a nice home, a family dog, private school, the works. To their credit, my folks produced a social worker (me), a data analyst (my sister Anita), and an autobody mechanic (my brother Joseph). Only stupid genes could account for Gonzo, the petty criminal.

It was less than a week until Christmas, the most joyous time of the year. As a family we should be baking cookies, maxing out our credit cards, and inviting friends to our Kwanzaa celebration. Instead, we were saying goodbye to Gonzo.

Gonzo wasn't his given name. It was Greg. We called him Gonzo after the Muppet character. He held onto the nickname as an adult because he thought it made him sound like a gangster. See? All. The. Stupid. Genes.

His stupidity was why the family gathered at Laclede's Landing, with the St. Louis Arch in the background. The day was crisp and sunny. The river smelled like old mop water. At least, it was a pleasant day to send his ashes into the Mississippi River. Poor Gonzo. He'd somehow gotten caught up in some illegal enterprise. His body ended up incinerated in a Lexus RZ on Grand Avenue.

My mother cried, for three days so far. I, as the oldest, had to hold things together. It was the hardest thing I ever had to do. My little brother—my stupid, funny, weird little brother—was so charred he had to be identified by his dental records. Worse, I knew something, or thought I knew something, or could've known something, that might have saved his life.

"And now we send Gregory 'Gonzo' Shipley to his home-going," the reverend said. "May he find the peace he searched for here on earth."

I took the urn to the edge of the water.

"No," my mother cried. "I'm not ready to let him go."

A brisk wind swept through the group, to penetrate every layer of clothing and send a chill to our bones. I could honor my brother's wishes or allow my mother additional time to mourn her youngest. Screw it. Gonzo's choices landed him in that car. He wasn't around to argue for his decision to be cremated and have his ashes scattered in the river. I handed the urn to my mother. "When you're ready, I'll take care of it."

"I don't understand how this happened." Mom swiped at her tears. "We did our best."

Genetics, I thought. Plato was right. Environment be damned. It had to be DNA. I patted my mother's hand and gave it a gentle squeeze. There was no point in telling her she'd done nothing wrong, unless it was producing an egg laden with chromosomes that turned a person, well, stupid.

After the repass, I returned home. In my bedroom, I removed the mysterious envelope from my supersecret hiding spot under the mattress. Gonzo gave it to me a week ago with strict instructions to not open it unless something happened to him. I couldn't make myself open it then and didn't want to now.

I sat on the bed with the sealed envelope clutched in both hands. Dare I open it? Maybe it'd be better to hold it over a candle. Whatever secret written within could be consumed by the flame. Gonzo had been so serious and so adamant when he handed it to me. I hadn't paid it the proper attention, because I didn't believe he was truly in any danger. Another aspect of Gonzo's personality was aggrandizement. I could never trust his assessment of anything. A girl he'd just met was the love of his life, for about a week. A traffic stop was a harrowing ordeal until you learned the officer was a five-feet-three woman who let him off with a warning. Words exchanged in a bar became a brawl. Gonzo was always...well, Gonzo. This time, it would seem, he'd had something to worry about.

He'd trusted me. I should honor his request and read his final words. I pulled out a sheet of paper and read.

Surprise! I'm not dead. Meet me in our secret place at 9 p.m. tonight. Tell no one. Make sure you're not followed. —G

This couldn't be real. As I considered the message, it became more probable. Gonzo was dumb enough to get into a situation that required him to fake his death, and foolish enough to try it. Ignoring the message was out of the question. I had to know. Hours remained before nine o'clock. My anxiety increased with each passing minute until my entire body ached from the strain.

At 8:00 p.m., I bundled up, got into my car, and drove around for forty minutes. I didn't know what the letter meant by 'make sure I wasn't followed'. If someone wanted to follow me, they would have to cross the Poplar Street Bridge into Illinois and return to Missouri via the Stan Musial Bridge. I would have noticed. I drove to our meeting place.

For the second time that day, I found myself headed to Laclede's Landing. Our secret place wasn't much of a secret. Whenever our parents took us to a baseball game, we'd beg to go to the Wax Museum. It never mattered how many times we went or how many times we viewed the same exhibits, the place fascinated us.

At 8:55, I stood in front of the entrance. I decided to give him five minutes past the appointed time. Part of me wanted this to be a useless endeavor. If Gonzo was alive, he wouldn't let the rest of us suffer. 9:05.

9:10. 9:15. At twenty minutes past, I gave up. It hadn't been real. He was gone.

"Psst, psst." From the shadows, a stout figure in a hoodie waved at me.

"Gonzo?" I asked.

"Shh." The figure waved again.

"I'm not following someone I don't know into a dark alley."

He pulled the hoodie back far enough to let me see his face.

I launched myself at him, intent on pulling Gonzo into a hug. Once I got close, my resolution shifted. I pounded him across his chest and head. "You... absolute... jackass."

"Stop hitting me. I can explain. Come on, Sis."

"You." Punch. "Better." Punch. "Have a damn good reason." Punch, punch. "For putting us through hell." I pulled the idiot into my arms and squeezed, tears streaming.

Gonzo patted my back. "We can't stay here. Follow me."

Farther down the alley sat a beat-up Chevy. We got in and Gonzo drove to an abandoned parking lot. "What took you so long? I've been waiting for you for days."

"I've been a little busy, just read your note." I glanced over my shoulder. "This isn't the safest spot."

"What does it matter? I'm already dead."

"Not funny. Tell me, what this is about."

Gonzo looked around as if a boogeyman might jump from the shadows. "Well, it started a couple weeks ago. I got an opportunity to make some quick money for the holidays."

"Gonzo," I groaned. I knew where the story was going. Over the years, he'd taken part in many pyramid schemes, frauds, and half-baked money-making opportunities.

"It was a simple job—low risk, high pay. All I had to do was deliver a package, receive something in return, and take the second package back. No effort for a big payday."

"Didn't Mom and Dad tell you a hundred times, if something sounds

68

too good to be true, it is?"

"But it wasn't! The job went exactly the way it was supposed to go."

"Then what went wrong, Gonzo?"

My little brother shifted in his seat and looked over his shoulder. "I didn't deliver the package exactly like it was given to me. It was a bag full of diamonds. Worth millions. I didn't think anyone would notice if I replaced them with high-quality fakes."

"Oh, Gonzo." The Stupid Gene struck again. "I assume you were dealing with a criminal. Somehow, you thought they wouldn't notice fake diamonds. Maybe there's still a way to get you out of this. I have money in savings, I can borrow from my retirement account, and there's a few grand I can draw from credit cards. How much to get you out of this?"

"Three million."

"Jesus, Gonzo!"

"That's why I had to fake my own death and go into witness protection."

"Then why are you here? Shouldn't you be in a safe house or something until you testify?"

"What are you talking about? I'm hiding at my friend Torrence's house. He's out of the country, so I figured it'd be a perfect place to lay low."

I pressed my thumb to my forehead in an attempt to ward off a headache. "Are you telling me you put yourself in witness protection?"

"Yes."

"That's not a thing."

"It is," Gonzo said with the absolute confidence of the chronically wrong. "Everyone thinks I'm dead. I'll disappear as soon as I get the diamonds. No one will see me again."

"Whose ashes are in the urn? The one mom's carrying around."

"I didn't kill anyone, if that's what you're asking. There was an unclaimed body in the morgue. Don't ask how I got it or how the medical examiner identified my body. You don't want to know. Let's say I was owed favors. Leave it at that."

I crossed my arms and stared at my brother. "What are you up to?"

"I want to get my life together. Things will be different this time. I'm going to Colorado to open a coffee and cannabis café. I just need your help. Please, Sis."

"What do you need me to do?"

"Pick up the diamonds and bring them to me."

"I'm not getting involved. For one, you're asking me to help you hide a crime. Two, you haven't thought things through, again. What happens when you try to sell your stolen goods? Whoever is looking for them, will find you and kill you."

"The diamonds are untraceable. That's what makes them so valuable. Unless they are moved, someone could get hurt. You can't let that happen."

"Where did you hide these diamonds?"

"At Mom's house."

If there had been a weapon in the car, I might have used it. "You placed something that could get someone killed in my mother's house?" I could barely get the words out, I was so furious.

"She's my mother, too. No one was supposed to know. The plan was to retrieve the diamonds before the explosion. If everything went well, when you showed up to meet me, no one would have been there. You would have thought the letter was a hoax. See? You were my backup plan. Please, Sis, please. Get the diamonds and bring them to me." He pulled out a restaurant business card with a number scribbled on the back. "Call me as soon as you have them. I'll tell you where to meet me."

"If I do this, you're going to leave?"

"I swear. Everyone will be safe."

"I'm doing this to protect mom. Tell me where to look."

* * *

It was late, almost 11, when I pulled up in front of the house. The scent of fried foods, cabbage, and pasta hit me as soon as I stepped onto the porch. Despite the late hour, mourners milled around, to share stories, and drink whiskey. I added my coat to a chair piled high with jackets and scarves, made my way through the crowd.

"Hey, Sis." Anita gave me a hug. "Didn't think we'd see you any more tonight."

"I wanted to check on mom."

"She's holding up. She's in the kitchen, making a good effort to give everyone diabetes by the end of the night."

I nodded and started towards the back of the house. Anita fell in step beside me.

"I'm going to miss Gonzo," she said. "He was fun. I can't remember when having him around didn't end in some kind of calamity. Remember the time we went camping? He convinced us we were supposed to leave food out for the bears to keep them from eating us."

I snorted. "We should have known better. It's not like we couldn't have asked mom or borrowed the computer to look it up. Why did we believe him?"

"Because he was so convincing," she said.

"We almost died."

"Almost." Anita waved her hand. "I did have the best story to tell about my summer vacation when I got back to school."

My fondness for Gonzo ripened under anger and frustration. He was, after all, my adorable kid brother. "Remember when he ran a gambling enterprise in high school? He made over ten-thousand dollars before being caught."

Anita shook her head. "Then, he convinced the principal he was raising money to help pay medical cost for the kid who got hit by a car. He handed the money over. All innocent and earnest."

I shook my head. "They rewarded him with a certificate of philanthropy. Hey, I've got one for you. Remember when he learned the word yeet? Yeet, yeet, yeet, everything was yeet!"

"I remember he yeeted his baseball through the neighbor's bathroom window. He almost scared Mr. Wilson to death since he was in there at the time. And when Mom made that big dinner and in the middle of it, Gonzo asked If I barf up my dinner, does that mean I yeeted my food?" Anita made a gagging face.

We looked at each other and burst into laughter.

"I have a confession," I said. "Gonzo didn't give all the money away. He gave me eight hundred dollars to keep my mouth shut."

"Eight hundred?" Anita said. "He only gave me two. How much money did he make?"

"We'll never know."

In the kitchen, we found Mom wrapping hunks of pound cake for people to take home.

"What's funny?" Mom asked.

"Gonzo stories," Anita said.

Mom nodded. "Such a sweet boy."

"Hey, Mom," Joseph said. "I heard someone ask Aunt Linda about your strawberry cake recipe."

Mom put a hand on her hip. "Let me put a stop to that. Linda is drunk enough to give away all my secrets. I better hide the family recipe book."

"I'll move it," I volunteered. "You take care of Aunt Linda. She's likely to curse someone out." Mom stored the family recipe book, the family Bible, and birth certificates in hat boxes. Since mom knew the recipes by heart, it made the perfect spot to hide a stash of diamonds.

"You're right" Mom said. "Make yourself a plate."

I went to mom's bedroom, moved her reading chair to the closet, and stood atop it. I dropped two large hat boxes to the floor before reaching the right one. I tucked the family cookbook under one arm and lifted a black velvet satchel. Curious, I poured the contents into my palm. I expected small carats and white stones. Instead, a mosaic of brilliant diamonds cascaded out of the bag. Each diamond was at least three carats, some five. Gonzo either lied when he told me about the gems or had underestimated their value. Knowing Gonzo, either or both options could be true.

I returned the diamonds to the satchel, tucked it into the waistband of my jeans, and smoothed my sweater over it.

"Is everything okay?" The question made me jump. My brother Joseph was behind me, a red cup filled with alcohol in hand.

"Don't do that." I held my hand to my chest. "You almost made me fall."

"Sorry. You want me to take care of that?" He pointed to the book under my arm.

"I got it." I climbed off the chair and moved it to its usual position. "Did you want something?"

"Yes." Joseph sat on the bed and patted the place beside him.

I hesitated. I needed to get back to Gonzo, but running out would look suspicious. "What's up?"

"You're taking this hard." Joseph let out a slow sigh. "I realize this comes off as sibling rivalry. Gonzo was everyone's favorite but stop talking about him like he was a mischievous kid. He was a grown man who got himself killed. I hate to say it, but it might have been for the best."

"Joseph!"

"You can't have forgotten Dad got shot in the shoulder when he tried to get Gonzo out of trouble. A few more inches, and he could have died long before the cancer took him. Have you forgiven Gonzo for Mom going into debt when she bailed him out of that real estate scheme? Sooner or later, his antics were going to harm us all."

"He's not a bad person. He never means to cause trouble. He just doesn't think things through." I caught myself using the present tense. "I meant he *didn't* think things through. He never found his way."

Joseph stared into the cup filled with ice half-melted by rum. "We never let him find his way, did we? We're partly responsible because we never let him learn his own lessons." He took a swig of his watered-down drink. "I wish the knucklehead was here. All I'm saying is, don't remember him through rose-colored glasses just because he's dead." Joseph patted my back and left.

I sat, thinking about Joseph's words. A realization came to me. I knew what I had to do. I pulled out the card Gonzo gave me earlier and made the call.

* * *

I stood on the Chain of Rocks Bridge, and gazed in the direction of the Gateway Arch, a silhouette against the dark sky. I heard a noise and jumped. Nothing. Probably the wind caused the bridge to creak. I didn't anticipate trouble, but no one goes to an isolated place in the middle of the night with good intentions. I stuck my hands into the pockets of my coat, wrapped my fingers around the velvet satchel, and waited.

A figure came into view. I recognized my brother from his confident stride. Gonzo was ten yards away when I called for him to stop.

"What's wrong?" Gonzo asked. "What took you so long?"

"I had to run an errand."

"You found my stash?"

I pulled the bag from my pocket, jiggled the contents, and held it where he could see it.

"Why did you want to meet here?" Gonzo asked.

"Couple of reasons. We couldn't chance meeting in any of our usual places. This seemed the perfect spot for illicit activities."

"You watch too much Dateline."

"Maybe, but this is the last chance I'll ever have to help you. Forgive me for wanting to add a little drama."

"I appreciate your help. Now give me the bag."

Gonzo took a step forward. I took a step back. "I have something to say. I want you to be a better person. I hope this is the start of that."

"It is. I promise."

Gonzo took another step forward. I took another step back.

"You've made a lot of promises in the past and broken every single one. I can't let you do it again. I can't let you break Momma's heart again. So, this is for your own good." I pivoted and lifted my arm. With as much strength as I could muster, I yeeted the velvet satchel into the Mississippi River.

Gonzo screamed my name. "What have you done? I can't escape

without money." Gonzo held his head and spun in a circle like a caged rat. "I'm dead, I'm dead, I'm *so* dead."

"You're not. I didn't throw them all." I dug into my other pocket, held out a small box, and shook it. "There are five diamonds in here. Not enough for the life of luxury you envisioned, but enough to buy yourself a last chance. Go to Colorado. Open your café."

I placed the box at my feet and walked backward a few yards. Gonzo had never been violent, but I'd never ruined his chance to convert stolen goods into millions of dollars.

He picked up the box and looked inside. "I can't believe you betrayed me. We're family. I'll never forgive you."

"That's okay. Just don't come back. If you do, I'll out you. I'll have to do it to protect the family. I love you, Gonzo. Be happy."

I waited until he'd gone before I went back to my car. I wished him all the luck in the world. He'd need it.

* * *

Two hours earlier

I sat on mom's bed and made up my mind. I called Gonzo, arranged our meeting. In the car, I removed a few diamonds from the bag and placed them in a box that once held a pair of candy cane earrings. Then I drove around the city.

My journey took me through our Benton Park neighborhood, Soulard, Lafayette Square, the Gate District, and Fox Park. I detoured through Dutchtown, Tower Grove, and the Central West End. I drove Downtown and circled twice through the streets of North St. Louis.

I'd made a plan to drive through all the working-class neighborhoods and now and again, yeet a stone out the driver's side window for people to find. But who would recognize a real diamond, especially the size and color of these? They'd likely go to waste.

I made a better plan.

I'd keep the diamonds. For myself.

I guess Gonzo didn't get All. The. Stupid. Genes. after all.

Magpie Baby
Vicki Erwin

July in St. Louis is hot. Being eight months pregnant is hot (in the temperature sense, not in the sexy sense). Even the Gateway Arch, massive as it is, cannot provide enough shade for the thousands of people who were downtown for the Fourth of July parade.

I held up my water bottle. "Empty," I said to my husband, Charlie, who had finally responded to the cries of our two-year-old, Lilibet, and hoisted her to his shoulders so she could see the parade that, at this point, seemed to have lasted several days.

"We'll get you some as soon as a vendor comes by," he said.

"Are you kidding? At five dollars a pop? No. Give me the card for your office. I'll fill mine while I enjoy the air conditioning." If I could bottle the sweat dripping off me, I would drink that.

Charlie looked at me like I was crazy. And I was, for agreeing to come downtown today.

"I have to work in the bar association raffle booth in twenty minutes. I don't have time to walk to the office and back."

"I'm a big girl." I patted my enormous baby bump. "Perfectly capable of walking alone, well, with Lilibet." I loved my little one, but being a mom was hard on a day like today.

"'Nother pretty, Mama. Gimme." Lilibet leaned to the side, unbalanced Charlie and made him stumble into the bearded man in a sleeveless t-shirt and cut-off shorts next to him. The man elbowed him. Charlie scooted closer to me, just what I didn't need in this heat.

I leaned down—ugh!—and picked up the Mardi Gras-style necklace thrown from the passing—and every other—parade float. This one was shiny silver, made in the same design as the jeweled fleur-de-lis necklace that was the main item in the bar association raffle to raise money for the Innocence Project. Whoever had that idea was a marketing genius. I heard the raffle talked about everywhere I'd gone the last few weeks. Everyone wore a copy of the necklace. Lilibet wore at least six.

Not only was the original necklace valuable because it was precious metal and real stones, but it had historical value. Supposedly, two early citizens of St. Louis fought a duel over it and the woman who wore it. The winner was an ancestor of Charlie's mentor at his law firm. He'd donated the necklace—and chosen Charlie to be in charge of the raffle.

I dropped the plastic fleur-de-lis over my toddler's head to join the others she'd already collected. Lilibet was a big fan.

The woman beside me frowned. I could almost read her thoughts. 'That baby is going to choke herself with one of those necklaces.' Yes, Lilibet put them in her mouth, but it was easier to watch what she was doing than say she couldn't do it. What the woman didn't know was my daughter is a little magpie who picks up every shiny object that comes her way. Necklaces were her favorite. Six months into this pregnancy, I'd given up trying to stop her from wearing them. It was at the point where she couldn't fall asleep without rubbing the beads between her fingers to calm herself. Of course, I worried she'd swallow a piece or catch a necklace on something and strangle herself. So, I watched her. Closely.

Charlie put Lilibet in her stroller and pulled his phone from his pocket. She immediately screamed in that way only a toddler can. "No ride! No ride. Walk. Out. Out. Out."

"Shh!" I uselessly tried to quiet her.

"Sh—I mean crap." Charlie held out his phone. "I've got to go. There's some emergency at the raffle booth."

As he turned, I grabbed his shirt. "Don't leave without giving me that keycard. And…what kind of emergency can there be at a raffle booth?"

"Didn't say. Probably ran out of tickets, the way they were selling earlier. I think Mr. Spencer will be very happy with how I've handled this." Spencer was the senior partner.

Charlie groaned as his phone buzzed a second time. "There's a police alert, too. A gang's loose in the crowd, grabbing valuables—necklaces, rings, bracelets—right off people's necks, fingers, arms. In broad daylight, in plain sight." He pulled away and looked around, his gaze resting on the gentleman—I use the descriptor loosely—who had elbowed him when they collided.

Charlie leaned toward me and whispered, "Maybe you should turn your engagement ring around."

The diamond and sapphire ring had been a gift when Charlie made partner in his law firm, the most valuable piece of jewelry I owned. I'd tried to take it off weeks ago, but my fingers were too swollen. I wanted to turn it around. Still too swollen. Let someone try to take it off. They'd be dragging me along with it.

"On second thought, maybe you should stay with me," Charlie said, a worried look on his face.

I waved my hand along my pregnant body. My face had to be an unattractive beet red and streaked with sweat. My hair felt like a disaster—strands either stuck to my cheeks and forehead or curled into corkscrew knots and sticking straight out. Anyone who looked at my swollen ankles would think I was related to Raja, the St. Louis Zoo's favorite elephant.

Charlie handed me his key card without another word. "You need it for the outside door, the elevator, and the entry to the office. Take the express elevator that bypasses the first 21 floors."

I nodded. Express sounded great. I wanted a bathroom, water, and to take my shoes off. Cool air and a comfortable couch would be icing on the cake.

I made no friends as I pushed the stroller through the horde to the Mercantile Tower. The crowd thinned as we moved away from the parade route. I stopped when Lilibet spotted another necklace. With a sigh, I squatted to pick it up. Still down, I struggled to stand up.

"Excuse me, but I think that's my necklace you're holding," a young man (younger than me, at least) said.

Before I could hand it to him, Lilibet grabbed it and draped it around her neck.

"I'm sorry," I said, still trying to stand.

The man reached to remove the necklace from my daughter's neck.

"Mine!" She screamed so loud and so shrill, I wondered if she'd shattered nearby windows. The few people around us turned to look.

He pulled his hand back like he feared having it bitten off and backed away.

"There are dozens like it all over the street." I tried to smile as I finally made it upright.

"But that one is mine. My, my…it has a special meaning," the man said.

I couldn't imagine what kind of special meaning a plastic necklace would have. I walked a bit faster toward the entrance to Charlie's office building. Once there, I juggled the stroller, my purse, and the diaper bag, trying to position the key card properly.

"Let me help you."

The man had followed me!

"I work here, and those cards can be tricky."

"Thanks," I managed to get out. My mouth was so dry from thirst— and a bit of alarm at his persistence over a cheap necklace—that I could barely speak.

Lilibet held her necklaces with tight fists.

I headed straight for the elevator and stuck the card in the slot. Having to use the bathroom was about to trump my thirst. The young man was right behind me.

Again, he held the door as I pushed Lilibet's stroller into the elevator.

"What floor?" I asked as I pushed 36.

"Me, me, me push!" Lilibet used her piercing shriek.

I pulled her out of the stroller while waiting for the man to answer.

"Thirty-four," he said.

I pointed, and Lilibet pushed, then punched the four buttons underneath that one before I swung her away from the panel. "Sorry," I said again as the toddler slid to the floor.

Although I'd never seen him, he must work for Charlie's law firm. The realization helped me relax slightly. The man carried a leather briefcase on a strap over his shoulder. He wore a pink golf shirt with a Pebble Beach logo and khaki shorts. He had a bushy mustache and a short beard. The summer stylings of a young associate.

"You work with my husband, Charlie Finn?"

"My daddy," Lilibet said. "Charlie." She moved over and grabbed the man's leg.

"Uh, yeah, I guess. At Talley, Spencer, and Shaw. I just started and haven't met everybody yet."

"What department?"

"Umm, estates and trusts."

"You probably don't know Charlie then. He's a litigator."

The man nodded, smiled weakly, and stared at the numbers over the door.

Lilibet licked his leg.

The man leaned down and unwound her arms from around his knees. "Go back to Mommy."

She licked him again. He swiped at the wet spot on his leg.

"Lilibet! Come over here."

"Why?" she said.

"It's not nice to lick people," I said.

"Why?" She licked him again and giggled.

I wanted to say because you don't know where that leg may have been, but instead, I answered, "They may not like it."

"Why?"

I knew this could go on for the entire length of the—with a clunk and a rattle, the elevator lurched to a stop.

Lilibet dropped to the floor and cried out. I steadied myself against the wall behind me, held onto my baby bump. I did not want him to be born today in, of all places, an elevator with a stranger and a screaming toddler in attendance. I waited for my life to flash in front of my eyes as the elevator plunged us to our deaths, but it remained steady and unmoving.

The man's bag slid off his shoulder as he stared at me.

"How pregnant are you?" he asked.

"Eight months plus." My nervousness about being stuck so near my due date was now shared with my elevator buddy.

His Adam's apple bobbed as he swallowed. "Better call for help," he said, and reached toward the red button.

"No!" Lilibet's cries quieted, and she scrambled to her feet. "Me push!"

There was no way I could pick her up again. "Could you help her reach the button?"

With a heavy sigh, he grabbed Lilibet under her arms like she might explode and held her toward the pad.

I pointed at the red alarm button this time, and Lilibet pushed. It rang loudly. She giggled and rang it again, then again, and again until the man plopped her on the floor. "No!" she screamed.

There was a phone that rang as soon as the alarm bell faded away. I answered. "We're stuck on elevator number 217, it looks like between floors 19 and 20," I said.

The man grabbed the phone from me. "With a pregnant woman." He listened. "Me and a kid. Yes. Okay. Hurry." He slammed the phone back into its hook. "They said they'll get here as fast as they can, but there's a lot of people downtown, and first responders are busy." He chewed his mustache.

I shrugged. At least it wasn't hot in the elevator. If there was only a chair.

"Water, Mama."

My thirst returned with a vengeance. "It's all gone."

Vicki Erwin

Lilibet stamped her foot. "Water, now."

"As soon as we get to Daddy's office."

She turned to the man. "Up!" Lilibet held her arms out.

"She wants you to pick her up," I said, fighting a smile. We may have ruined the possibilities of fatherhood for this man forever.

"Mush-tache Man, up!"

Like a very good although reluctant sport, he picked up my daughter. He could be thinking about his status as an associate and Lilibet's dad's as a partner. She thanked him by grabbing onto his mustache and pulling. He jerked back, and I'd swear the mustache pulled away from his skin, then moved closer to his lip. Hmm. He smoothed it down.

"What's your name?" I asked. "I'm Meghan. Might as well get acquainted. No telling how long we'll be here."

"Tom," he said, sliding Lilibet to the floor. "I have a bottle of water here if you want…"

"Water, Mama!" Lilibet said.

Tom opened his bag and pulled out a water bottle.

I was grateful to see it was unopened when he handed it to me. I took Lilibet's cup out of our bag, poured some into it, gave it to her, and then took a long drink out of the bottle. Ignoring the water she'd wanted so badly, Lilibet squatted beside the leather briefcase and had her hand inside.

When she pulled her hand out, she held onto a sparkly gold and diamond bracelet. "Pretty," she said.

It certainly was pretty and looked very expensive.

"That's mine," Tom said and held out his hand.

"No!" Lilibet placed it on top of her head.

He looked at me. "That's two pieces of jewelry your child has stolen from me. I wonder if she isn't the 'grab and go bandit' the police put out an alert about."

I leaned toward his bag. Lilibet had pulled out a black hoodie and a stocking cap. My stomach—not my uterus—clenched. No one needed either of those on a day like today.

Tom kicked the bag behind him, and a gold chain and a ruby ring shot across the floor.

Lilibet was faster than he was and grabbed them. She put the gold chain over her head, knocked the bracelet to the floor, then spun the ring around one of her tiny fingers. Tom scooped up the bracelet.

"Mine!" she said.

"Mine," Tom repeated and stuck it in his pocket. He glared at me, and I picked up Lilibet and pressed into the corner of the elevator.

I was getting a bad vibe.

"No, Mama. Down!"

She squirmed, wiggled, and kicked until I set her on the floor but held onto the strap of her sundress.

"Out! I want out!" Lilibet leaned toward the door and pulled away. The ruby ring bounced across the floor, and again, she grabbed it before Tom. She stuck her tongue through it and wiggled it at us.

Omigod. If she swallowed that ring…

Tom and I reached for her at the same time, and our heads cracked together. Lilibet laughed as we rubbed the points of collision.

"Again!" she said, the ring slipping off her tongue.

Tom was fastest this time, drying it on his shorts, a disgusted look on his face. He placed it in his pocket.

The baby inside me kicked me in the bladder. "Oof!" I grabbed my abdomen and leaned forward, placing my hand against the wall to keep my balance.

"What!" Tom's face paled by two or three shades.

"I need a bathroom like five minutes ago."

"Go potty, Mama?" Lilibet squatted. "Diaper icky. Out," she said.

"We can't get out," Tom said, each word sharp as a knife. "Don't you think I'd be gone if we could?"

Lilibet leaned her head to one side and looked up at him. "Why?" she said.

He shook his head.

"Diaper off." She reached under her dress and had her diaper off before I could stop her. It dropped at Tom's feet.

"This is a nightmare," he said.

"Lay down, baby," I said, lowering myself to my knees. It was even money whether the first responders would find me stuck in this position when they showed up. I could say I was praying. And maybe I should be.

Pulling her dress up, Lilibet announced, "I don't have a penis."

"For the sake of …" Tom shook his head.

He, a guy who, by my reckoning, could be a common thief, had the nerve to judge me. And still, I defended myself. "I didn't teach her that," I said. "She learned it at Mother's Day Out." Besides being a magpie, Lilibet repeated everything she heard.

"Turn off light!" Lilibet closed her eyes and moved her head from side to side. As she shifted, the light caught on one of the necklaces, and it sparkled more, and differently, than the others. It sent a hint of rainbow across the ceiling of the elevator.

Again, my stomach clenched. I ran my finger over the stones in the fleur-de-lis necklace Tom claimed was his. They were bevel-set, and the metal cold, not paste, not plastic.

How could I not have noticed? Blame it on the heat? Pregnancy brain? Lack of attention? Tom was worse than the "grab and go" bandit. He'd managed to steal the prize from Charlie's raffle.

The emergency phone rang again, and I reached for it, hoping to somehow hint at who was in the elevator with me. Tom batted my hand away and answered.

"The fire department is on the way. Maintenance tried to fix it here but couldn't," he informed me.

I closed my eyes and sat back on my heels.

"You know who I am, don't you?" Tom said.

I said nothing as I placed Lilibet's diaper in a plastic bag and stuck it in the carry-all.

"May I have my necklace now?"

"Mine," Lilibet said and clasped her necklaces tightly.

"No matter what you think you saw or think you know, it's in your best interest to say nothing. And to get that necklace from Red Chief." This time, his voice was colder.

At least the man was a reader. He had to be referring to the O. Henry story, "Ransom of Red Chief." Made me proud of my little girl.

Before I could, Tom picked up my daughter.

"Hi, Mush-tache Man," she said. Lilibet grabbed a piece of his hair and twisted.

"Ow!" Tom pulled away, and when he did, Lilibet's fingers were covered in something dark and sticky.

She held her hand to her mouth, and that gave me the impetus I needed to pull myself to standing. I grabbed her hand away. Lilibet wiped what must have been temporary hair color onto Tom's (I was pretty sure that wasn't his name) shirt. Then she grabbed his mustache and pulled. Her eyes were as round as the elevator alarm button when the lip fuzz came off. Lilibet shook her hand several times, then the fake mustache flew across the elevator.

In a gesture of defeat, Tom pulled off the beard as well and dropped it in his briefcase.

"What if we trade necklaces?" Tom said. He pulled three sets of Mardi Gras beads out of his pocket. "Look! I'll give you all these, and you give me one necklace." He placed his finger under the original.

Lilibet shook her head. "Purple," she said.

"No, these are red and green," Tom said.

"Purple," Lilibet said louder.

If I hadn't been so frightened, I would have laughed or at least smiled. Never argue with a toddler.

Tom looked toward me with a frown. "No, red." He held up a red necklace. "And green." He held up the other necklaces.

"Purple," Lilibet shouted right into his face.

"She wants a purple one," I said.

"I don't have a purple one." He looked behind him like one might suddenly appear.

There was a knock on the elevator doors. "Fire department."

"Thank heaven," I said. "We're here, we're still...."

"My wife and daughter need to get out of here." Tom pinned me with eyes that were dark and hard. He shifted Lilibet to his other arm. "Meghan is pregnant, eight months," he added.

Murmurs followed Tom's lie.

"I'm fine," I said. "Just need to *GRAB* some water and *GO*."

"Don't say another word," Tom said in what would have been a hiss if there were any ssss to hiss.

"We're working as fast as we can," a woman's voice said.

"We'll go to your husband's office, and I'll take the necklace once we're alone. If you say anything..."

"How did you manage to steal that necklace?" Charlie had been so careful about security.

Tom looked proud as he explained. "Once I staged a few grab and goes, the police spread out to find me, left the raffle booth manned by rent-a-cops. Made it much easier."

I couldn't let him take the necklace. He'd admitted he was the "grab and go bandit." And the necklace he was so anxious to have... I ran my finger along it, more determined than ever to keep it from him. My husband's future might be at stake.

"You aren't even a lawyer, are you?"

Tom laughed.

There was a screech as the door opened, then a ladder dropped.

Tom quickly sat Lilibet on the floor and grabbed the ladder.

I groaned as liquid gushed between my legs, splashing Tom and causing him to back away.

"What the hell..."

"No cursing in front of the baby," I said.

"Excellent timing," one of the first responders said, taking in the liquid running across the floor. "Let's get her out of there."

Tom grabbed the ladder again and was on the second rung when the firefighter pushed him off. "Hey, buddy, let us get to your wife."

"Come to me, Lilibet," Tom said.

Lilibet held up her arms.

"No, no, baby. Stay here with Mama."

Tom grabbed Lilibet around the waist. "Let me move her out of the way."

"Don't! Don't…"

"Is there something going on here?" A police officer popped his head around the three firefighters and asked.

"My necklace," Lilibet said, grasping all those around her neck in her little fist. She glared at Tom.

I won't say anything, I mouthed. Let her go.

The female firefighter descended the ladder. "Hey, Daddy, give me the baby." She stared at Tom. "You're wearing some hefty jewelry there," she said to Lilibet.

"Not Daddy. Mush-tache Man," Lilibet grabbed a handful of Tom's hair. "Icky." She held out her hand stained with hair dye, wiped it on Tom's shirt again, and giggled.

The firefighter looked unsure what was happening as she turned to me. "Can you make it out by yourself? Are you having labor pains?"

Before I answered, the "grab and go" thief thrust the baby toward the female firefighter, threw her off balance. He grabbed at Lilibet's necklaces.

She kept her tiny fist closed tight around the beads. "No, no, Mush-tache Man. Mine," she yelled at him.

Tom made a sudden move toward the ladder. His shoe hit the mustache Lilibet had pulled off his face, now floating in liquid. His leg slid out from under him, and he landed in a half-split, his face pale. He held his ankle and groaned. "Out, I want out of here. Away from that devil child."

This time, I grabbed the ladder and climbed upward. The water bottle slid out from between my legs and dropped to the elevator floor.

"He's the "grab and go" thief," I said. "Check his bag and pockets."

"That kid stole necklaces from me," Mustache-Man-Tom said hotly as a police officer cuffed him.

"We need to get you to the hospital," the firefighter said to me as paramedics unfolded a gurney.

"I need medical attention, too," the thief called. "I think my damn ankle is broken."

"Shh! No cursing in front of the baby." I fought to keep my laughter from bubbling out. I turned to the first responders gathered around me. "I'm fine. That was water, I mean bottled water. I needed something to keep your attention on bringing me out before he escaped."

"I can see where she gets it," the female firefighter said. She looked from me to Lilibet, who removed one of her necklaces and dropped it over the woman's head.

The thief, formerly known as Tom, glared over his handcuffs at us.

"All we need is to go upstairs, go to the bathroom, and rest awhile," I assured the first responders.

The female firefighter continued to try to convince Lilibet to give up the jeweled necklace. She tried trading for a fire captain badge and more Mardi Gras necklaces, but nothing would convince my magpie baby to loosen her grasp on the real thing. Whenever someone, including me, tried to pry her fingers loose, she screamed bloody murder. Our ears rang.

When Lilibet finally fell asleep from what I believed to be exhaustion, the necklace came off and was returned, under police escort, to the raffle display.

One of the headlines in the digital edition of the St. Louis Post-Dispatch later in the day was: "Magpie Baby Outsmarts Grab and Go Thief," Lilbet's first appearance in the newspaper. The big news was Magpie Baby Lilibet became big sister to Firecracker Baby Liam, born early, but healthy at 10:08 pm on the Fourth of July. And yes, she tried to gift said brother with a purple (it was red) fleur-de-lis necklace, which was promptly removed from his bassinet.

Waverly, My Love
Glen Bush

The key beneath the cactus outside my window was gone. Waverley must be inside, probably watching TV. Walking in, I could hear two distinct sounds. One was the television. The second was a low primeval moan. I peeped around the corner into the living room. It was primeval all right, damn near the oldest human sound ever made, that soft, low moan that comes from unadulterated sex.

Waverley was on some guy's lap, her legs planted firmly on each side of his. He sat in my favorite desk chair. I couldn't see much of him. Her body covered him like a dark cashmere topcoat. She pulled his head toward her breasts and buried his face. Her dark brown, naked back, wide shoulders that tapered to a narrow waist, blended seamlessly with her muscular, flexing derriere. She leaned her head back, parallel with the ceiling, and stared at the slow moving ceiling fan. Her moans came in a slow rhythm that synced perfectly with her contorting buttocks.

This was my apartment, but this wasn't my place. I stepped back and returned to the porch. I left the door cracked so I could hear when the groans stopped. Unfolding my lawn chair, I settled down and began to check the odds Jimmy the Nose was giving on the Lakers game. I texted the Nose to put a hundred down. Eventually, the moaning stopped, but being the easily embarrassed type, I waited before I went inside.

Standing on the threshold, I saw Waverley naked, her back to me, and some guy, twenty-something, with the body of an ex-high school football player, ready to pick up his red and white checkered shirt.

Damn! He's the pizza delivery driver!

Spotting me, he yelled as though this were his house, "Who the hell are you? What are ya doin' starin' at us?"

Before I could respond, Waverley turned, gave me a big smile, and said, "Hello, Quinn, you're home early. You said you wouldn't be here 'til midnight. Hope you don't mind, but I got hungry, so I ordered a pizza, and..." It was obvious Waverley had either forgotten the guy's name or, most likely, never knew it. "And... the pizza guy and I decided to satisfy our natural urges. You don't mind, do you?"

"Nah, Waverley, it's all good." Then, I told him to take a hike.

"Hey, you don't tell me what to do. My girl and me may not be finished." Tough was not his gift. The guy was trying to talk tough. Waverley shook her head, looked at him, then at me, and gave me her 'don't-hurt-him-too-badly' grin.

I saw fear in his eyes. What the hell, I slapped him on the ear. "Get out, kid. Do yourself a favor, forget this address and phone number. Got it?"

Waverley blew him the kiss, and said, "Go on, boy, and thanks for the pizza."

He hesitated, wanted to say something macho, but again, failure. The words didn't exist in his lexicon.

After he was gone, and Waverley had put her pants and tee shirt on, we sat at the table, popped a couple of beers, and began to eat the pizza.

"Waverley, what the hell was that all about?"

"Come on, Quinn, you never had the urge to clap cheeks?"

"Yeah, plenty, but not in somebody else's apartment with the pizza girl. Damn!"

"Quinn, don't get cheugy on me. If you can do it, why in the hell can't I? Who made the rule men can screw whenever but women can't? That is soooo old!"

"Waverley! Waverley, I don't know anything about rules concerning who's screwing who or when. I'm just sayin'..."

"You know, Quinn, a long time ago, I had a Korean girlfriend. She used to sometimes look at me and out of the clear blue say, 'Me so horny, Waverley, me so, so horny.' Then she would just fuck like a mink. Well, I decided right then and there that's how I would look at my sex life. Just straight bang! If you stop and think a minute, you know all the time you've known me, all the missions we've been on, I've never thought about anything else but the job. Only the job. One hundred percent. When the job is over, and if I want to get a little R & R, maybe hookup, I damn well will do it and I don't need your permission. Okay, Quinn?"

I'd never heard Waverley talk this much since I'd known her. Like she said, one hundred percent business. I had no right to interfere in her personal life. A couple more beers and we decided to get back to why I asked her to come over in the first place.

"Okay, got it. Let's talk."

Waverley passed her hand in front of her face as if wiping away anything that may be blinding her, and now all business, said, "I'm all ears."

* * *

"East of Tower Grove Park, there's three blocks of mom-and-pop shops. Before goin' into the Army, I used to hang out in the diner and play pinball there. Well..."

"Mallory's Diner?"

The question caught me off guard. "Yeah, Mallory's, but how'd you know?"

"What? You don't think a black girl from the Compton Projects would know Mallory's, the best damn place in the city for Danish? We moved there from the Projects about the time you went into the Army. So, go on, tell me, what's going on at the diner?"

"Small world. You never told me."

"No reason. We all come from somewhere." Waverley was back in her matter-of-fact mode.

I went on, "Then y'know how tight those storekeepers, owners, and the neighbors are around there. The bottom line is, Chet Mallory reached out to me, said his niece is missing. Been gone for about a week. He went to the police, made the missing person report, but nothing. Seems like some banger's been rousting him and a few others around Tower Grove East. When someone doesn't pay up, things get damaged, sometimes people. I told Chet to call the police again. A few did, but the police said there was nothing to link the banger to anything. The ones payin' off ain't talkin'. So, I told him I'd check it out. I'm thinkin' this is a case where I'm gonna need help. I called you."

"Who's the banger?"

"Black guy, ex-con, they call him Rabbit. Tyrese Holt. He's…" Before I could go further, Waverley stopped me.

"When did he get out?"

"Last year 'round Christmas. Y'know him?"

"Yeah, I know him. I'd like to yeet his ass into next week."

The look in her eyes let me know that her and Holt were not BFFs.

"How much info do you have on this?" Leaning toward me, she went on, "You see, Quinn, Rabbit likes certain kinds of girls, so if he's got her, well, he's not playing Sesame Street." She stopped for a moment and squeezed the Bud Light can tight. "He's sent a lot of folks from the projects to the funeral home. When he went to prison, I hoped some con would shank his ass. Looks like that didn't happen. Since my mother died, I don't go back there. Rabbit was still in Ironwood then. Twenty to twenty-five. He either got out on parole or maybe his lawyer found a loophole. Anyway, looks like he's moved west toward the park. Always looking for fresh meat."

Waverley got up and walked around the room, looked for something that was not missing, killed time, held back the tears that wanted to escape.

"You wanna talk about it? What he did to you?"

"Nah, I don't want to ever talk about him or those times. If that changes, I'll let you know."

"You wanna skip this case? I can get…"

"I don't skip cases because of ghetto trash like Tyrese Holt."

"Well, then, why don't I lay out what I got, and we can then piece together a plan?"

"Let's do it."

* * *

We sat across the booth from Chet Mallory in his diner. He remembered Waverley from the past so they exchanged greetings and a few memories. Chet had even been a pallbearer at her mother's funeral. The waitress brought us coffee and Danish. Mallory stuck with water. It was now almost ten days since Mallory had seen his niece, Selena.

"She's fifteen years old. Blonde. A beautiful Irish Latina who wants to be a wildlife biologist."

When Mallory told me that, my cynical side couldn't help but think she may be getting schooled in another type of wildlife, the kind Waverley and me hunted.

Selena's parents, he said, spent their time going back and forth to the police, to beg them to arrest Rabbit. Her father, Devin, had almost been arrested because he confronted Rabbit on the street. If it hadn't been for a sympathetic cop with a dead daughter, Devin Mallory would have been in City lockup. We weren't surprised by Chet's story. What we needed now, though, was the when and where of Selena Mallory.

"The last time Holt came here to the diner, Selena was workin' the cash register. He started talkin' to her as soon as he came in. Y'know, that street talk, about money and bling and all the crap he could do for her if she'd just stop punching the cash register buttons and come with him." The more Mallory talked, the more I thought he was going to break the water glass he was squeezing. "Anyways, I come up and asked him what he wanted. That's when he told me he sells insurance. At first, I didn't know what he meant, but then he says some thugs could start terrorizing my diner and maybe Selena, too. For five hundred a week, he could make everything safe. I straight up told him thanks, but no thanks, and that's when he looked at Selena, looked at her with his damn snake eyes, smiled, then turned back to me and asked if I was real sure about that. He had two of his thugs standing at the front door watchin' everything. That's the last I saw of him. Two days later, Selena was gone." The water glass shattered.

Chet handed Waverley a photo of Selena in her volleyball uniform. Waverley studied the photo like she was looking into a mirror, raising her eyes, she continued her examination looking into the old man's face, and, finally, she studied the diner. After looking out the window for a moment, she turned back to him, lay her hand on his, the bloody one he had broken the glass with, and said, "I promise you, Mr. Mallory, if Holt has her, I'll bring her back to you." Over the years, I'd never heard her promise an outcome about a case. She'd always been logical, calculating, and as cold ass mean as a Chinese Dragon Lady.

When we were back in the car, I asked her, "Why'dya promise Mallory you'd find her? Y'know as well as me there's a good chance she's at the bottom of the Mississippi."

"I will bring her back. I told you, Quinn, I know Rabbit. I was one of his victims. He plays with his girls. He's one low-rent bastard. I'm guessing prison only made him more so. My worry is what kind of mental shape will Selena be in when we do get her. It's been almost two weeks. That's a long time to be in his hands. He knows how to live rent free in a girl's head. The police found me after only three days, and I was messed up. Funny, Quinn, the A.D.A. plea bargained my case out so they could get Holt to flip on some downtown drug dealer. Strange. You know what I'm saying?"

"Yeah, I know." Looking out the window of my Audi, Coltrane on the radio, I thought how I knew exactly what Waverley meant. It had always been that way, and it wasn't gettin' any better.

Waverley and I decided to split up. I'd go see Devin and his wife, Rosalita, and stop by the precinct later. She'd go talk to a few people from the block. Luckily for us, Tyrese Holt wasn't a gangsta who tried to win neighborhood favor by taking care of people in need. There was only one need, his personal trifecta, money, power, and revenge. That, I hoped, would work to our advantage.

* * *

Devin and Rosalita Mallory owned a cleaners a few blocks from Mallory's Diner. When I walked in, it looked like they expected me. Both walked out from behind the counter and guided me to the small office in the corner. Rosalita poured three cups of coffee and handed me one.

"It's fresh. I made it about thirty minutes ago. Chet said you'd be stopping by. Cream or sugar?"

"Black's fine." Devin pointed to a worn stuffed chair in the opposite corner. I guessed it was his chair. As I settled into the worn spot, Devin pulled his swivel desk chair toward me. Rosalita eased herself into the padded chair next to him. I could cut the fog of pain with my buck knife. It weighed us down. I tried to pretend like it was already over with, a done deal, history. Selena was at the diner, ringing up lunch tabs, saving up for college but wanting something isn't the way it is on the streets. Beyond that front door, it is what it is, and wanting and wishing ain't a part of the program.

"Do you think you can help us, Mr. Quinn?" Rosalita's words were direct but hopeful. Her eyes were dry. She had shed all her tears. Now all she had was a mother's dryness. Devin didn't say anything. He waited for me.

I didn't wanna screw this up. I figured I'd tell'em the truth.

"Me and Waverley are gonna do everything we can to get Selena back. Waverley's knows Rabbit from the past." I didn't see the need to share anymore of Waverley's story. "She's over in his neck of the woods talkin' to a few people who may be able to help. If they're gonna talk, they'll talk to her, not a cop or me. But before ya get your hopes too high, I'm telling you straight up, this is dangerous. Rabbit is a mean son-of-a-bitch. I'd like to just shoot his ass and get it over with, but that wouldn't guarantee us gettin' Selena back. For now, I need to know if you remember anything around the time she went missing or since that seems to not sit right with either of you."

The conversation went as I expected, nowhere. Selena was here.

Selena was gone. After a few more assurances, I told'em I'd keep them posted. Everything I said was the truth, I just didn't tell'em I expected we'd find her decomposing body, not their cheerful daughter.

* * *

My contact at the precinct was out on medical leave. That left me to talk to the usual cops. I knew most of them, but none well enough to call a friend. After a little checking, I found out Detective Steve Hillman was handling the case, a missing persons, not a kidnapping.

"Detective, mind if I ask why this is not a kidnapping?"

"Well, smart guy." Tilting his head back and rolling his eyes let me know Hillman wasn't going to be too interested in anything I might ask or say. "You see, for this to be a kidnapping, there has to be a kidnapping, y'know, like the girl being snatched up off the street and held some place. After that, then this so-called Mr. Kidnapper goes and contacts the family and says he wants some money, or the girl get whacked. But this hasn't happened. The girl's just gone, like here today, gone tomorrow, gone. Probably ran away. Got sick of workin' that five-and-dime job at a diner. Blame her? I seen her picture. Nice lookin' kid. Why's she wanna spend her life pushing cash register buttons? Huh? Why?"

"True, you could look at it that way, but my point is, Tyrese Holt's been leaning on Mallory and most of them shopkeepers along the avenue. He's not only got a rep for likin' young girls, but his sheet says he did time. Did you talk to Holt?"

"Actually, Quinn, we did. I didn't personally, but one of the patrolmen assigned to the neighborhood did. Said Holt was clean. He's got an airtight alibi for that time."

As soon as Hillman said that time, those little hamster wheels in my head started to turn double-time.

"Alibi for that time? What time? How do you know when she went missing? Somebody see her walk out the door and not walk back? When was that?"

"Nah, I just mean, from what we was told, she left work and never came home. She was walking toward the bus stop. So, one plus one always equals two. Don't worry, Quinn, kids like that always run away. They think they wanna be grown and do grown up shit, but they find out pretty damn quick it ain't no fun being grown. She'll walk herself right back through the front door. Believe me, I've been doin' this for fifteen years. I know these kids."

With that, Hillman stood up and started to put on his jacket. "Sorry, Quinn, but I've got a meeting with the captain about some county kids getting lost here on the South Side. Call me if you want my help with anything else."

As he walked away, I nodded and said, "Thanks, Steve." You could cut my sarcasm with a plastic knife. With Hillman gone, I was anxious to hear what Waverley found. Hopefully, more than me.

* * *

Back in my office, the sun behind the skyline, Waverley played with her gin and orange juice. I was doing pretty damn good on my wagon sipping my coffee. The fifth of Bombay gin and the quart of Florida OJ sat on the high coffee table behind her, next to my coffee pot and empty double rocks glass. The sparkling clean ashtray sat next to the glass. I was a good boy.

"Quinn, I think I have something. Mabel Mapes, better known to my generation as Mama June Bug, remembers Rabbit taking a young light skin girl, probably either white or Latina, out of his SUV last weekend. Friday night, maybe midnight or thereabouts. He was with two other jokers. They were going down the gangway that runs along side his liquor store. Mama June Bug said the girl looked drunk, maybe drugged. Either way, she wasn't a happy-go-lucky teenager. When I showed her the picture of Selena, she said she couldn't be sure. It was dark and whoever it was, was walking in between the three men. In any case, it's a little more than we had this morning. I did go over to the liquor store. There's an eight-foot chain link gate at the head of the gangway with a padlock. I went into the store, an old head was playing checkers with the clerk, a guy called One-Eye. He wore a black patch over his left eye. I showed the picture to them. Nothing. Bullshit, I got that pain in my gut that told me they knew something they didn't want to share."

Chewing on the ice from her drink, she waited for my response. I let the information roll around in my head for a couple ticks. Selena could be anywhere tonight. Rabbit could have moved her a dozen times between last Friday and tonight. Waverley didn't say anything more. She was content to wait. She did, though, get up and mix herself another drink.

"Waverley, by chance, did Mama June Bug say anything else about the neighborhood, y'know, anything about how things might have changed or be changin' since Rabbit's return? Maybe a change to a house or building? Y'see what I'm gettin' at is, Mr. Holt may be expanding his business opportunities. Gambling? Girls? Street shit. Liquor store and strip joints are pretty common for guys like Holt, but if he's thinking about going bigger than he was, he'll need some place else, some place bigger. Do you remember anything like that from the past?"

"The closest thing I can think of is, Mama said he was fixin' up the house behind the liquor store. Want to see what's there?"

"Might as well, I can't dance."

* * *

Near sunset, things looked dead in the neighborhood. Waverley played lookout. I used my growing-up skills to pick the padlock on the gate. As we walked into the gangway, shadows fell on us making it more cavern than walkway. At the end, a small brick yard with a tall sycamore separated the back of the liquor store from the two-story building facing the alley. Sitting on the steps of the backyard building were three men, all in their late twenties, smoking a joint and drinking from a brown paper bag. They didn't see us, so we leaned back to see what they might be up to besides getting high and waiting for the night. When one of them stood and walked over to the sycamore to piss on its massive trunk, Waverley whispered it was Rabbit. She gave me a wink and motioned I should step back, against the brick wall, deeper into the shadow. Puzzled, I went along with her idea. It wasn't until a few seconds later I realized it was a dumbass idea.

As she walked from the shadows into the dying beams of sunlight circling the sycamore, I slipped my Glock from my waistband and waited, thinking she really was some kind of woman.

* * *

"Hello, Rabbit, remember me?" Waverley's voice was a calm, cool, monotone that drew all three men's attention to her.

One of the men still on the steps, the one with the joint, jumped with surprise and half yelled, "Who da fug you?"

The other man remained quiet and still, watching Waverley and Rabbit, his right hand on his lap, inches from the handgun tucked in his belt.

Rabbit turned so he faced Waverley. Zipping his pants, he smiled, showed his gold grill.

"Wha' up, BBG? Hey, K.T., this here shawty is one of my firs' gurls from back in the day. Ya miss yer daddy, Baby Girl?"

"No, Rabbit, I can't miss ghetto trash."

"So, so mean. Why'ya wanna be like dat? Y'know ya can come home to daddy any time ya want. By the way, Mama June Bug told me ya was home axin' 'bout me and Selena. Why didn't 'cha jest come to daddy and ax me 'stead of sneakin' 'round like some wannabe female cop? Huh, Baby Girl? Why didn't 'cha?"

"Where is she? Where do you have Selena?"

Rabbit started to walk toward Waverley, his hands dropped to his sides. I didn't see a piece in his belt, but there was a good chance he had one, probably tucked into the small of his back. Waverley raised her Sig 9 mil and pointed it at him.

"Don't take another step, Rabbit, or it'll be your last." The ice in her voice told Rabbit the truth of the day.

The thugs hadn't seen me yet, so I figured we still had the upper hand. The two men on the steps didn't see it that way. The one sitting yelled for Rabbit to duck. Both fired at Waverley while Rabbit stooped behind the sycamore. Waverley hit the ground.

The next five seconds were a replay of the OK Corral. Ricochets and echoes filled the yard. Rabbit fired several rounds at Waverley first, then seeing me, tried to pick me off. In all the commotion and seeing his two henchmen lying at the foot of the steps, Rabbit leaped over them and ran into the brick building. The shooting stopped. Waverley and me looked at one another, nodded and moved toward the steps. Neither of us had been hit. Walking past the sycamore, I didn't see any blood drops.

"Doesn't look like Holt was hit either, no blood around here." I pointed to the ground around the tree.

"Not yet," said Waverley.

I picked up two handguns next to the two dead guys, put the Ruger in my belt and handed the Smith to Waverley. She slid it in her waistband.

"Let's go see who's in the house."

"Let's."

* * *

The living room was on the right. What had once been a parlor, on the left. The darkened hallway took us toward the kitchen where I could see a gas stove in the distance. There were two more rooms, one on each side, before we got to the kitchen. As we cleared the next room on the right and headed to the one across the hall, we heard muffled cries of "Help" come from behind the door. The door was unlocked.

Tied to the headboard with zip ties, wearing a torn tee-shirt and grimy sweatpants, was Selena, her face cut and bruised, lips swollen enough so it was difficult for her to speak. As we walked in and Waverley cut the zip ties, the tears ran down the teenager's face, her eyes wide with pain and fear.

"Waverley, take care of her while I go and find Holt. Call 9-1—"

"No, Quinn, you call 9-1-1, I'll go get Rabbit. Remember, I'm the one who made the promise." She put a full clip into her Sig and slipped the partial into her back pocket. Then she was gone. I could hear her open a door in the kitchen. It didn't sound like the back door, probably to the basement. These old rowhouses always had basement doors off the kitchen.

I called 9-1-1, requested an ambulance for Selena, and reported the two dead thugs in the yard.

While I washed Selena's face with a cool washrag and watched the EMT crew rush into the house, I heard one barely audible gunshot, like it came from the basement. As Selena was wheeled out, Waverley walked in. She wore her signature sense of contentment, common after a mission.

"Do we need to keep lookin' for him or did'ya find him?"

"Forget about it. No one will ever have to look for him again." Before I could say anything else, Waverley walked toward the EMT crew and Selena. "Quinn, why don't you call Selena's folks and ride with her to the hospital, I'll meet you there. I need to tell Chet the promise is kept."

Looking at my partner, I knew she was right. This case was hard on me, and I was used to street trash hammerin' decent folk, but for Waverley, it was, well... really fucked up.

* * *

At the emergency entrance, as I watched Selena taken inside, her parents beside her, a cop from the shooting scene started to question me.

"Why didn't you tell us about the third body in the basement? You didn't even mention the guy with the bullet hole in his forehead. Why not?"

I could tell he was pissed. Like he seemed to think I tried to hide a dead body. I did what I do with cops I don't know, I smiled.

"Sorry, Officer, I was thinking more about Selena, our kidnap victim, than the dead thugs littering their hideout. Forgive me?"

My sarcasm only irritated him more, but he bought my story.

* * *

By the time Selena was safe in her hospital room, her parents at her side, and the police were done with me and Waverley, it was almost dawn.

"Well, Waverley, looks like this case has not turned out as bad as it could have. Selena's going to need a lot of treatment, but she's a South Side girl, tough. She'll make it."

"Yeah, she'll make it. I'll look in on her, help her out. I like her parents, I like her whole family. Liam, you know you can call me my first name, Tina, you don't always have to call me Waverley, y'know?"

"Tina? Ummm, cute name. A little girlish for you, ain't it?"

"Fuck you, Quinn."

"Okay, okay! I gotcha. Tina, as in Tina Waverley. So, Tina, you wanna get some breakfast?"

"Thanks, Quinn, but I think I'll head home. Catch you later, alligator." She leaned toward me, pulled my head down, and kissed me on the cheek. "Bye."

* * *

I decided to make my own breakfast at home. My scrambled eggs and bacon are better than my local greasy spoon. Since I was sober and hungry, I figured I'd cook for myself. About halfway through my meal, the doorbell rang. Seven-thirty in the a.m. Who in the hell rings anybody's doorbell at seven-thirty? When I opened the door, Tina was there. It didn't look like she'd been home. Same clothes. Same smudged face. Carrying a white bag of Danish from Mallory's Diner.

"Waverley! I mean, Tina, what the hell?"

"Me so, so horny."

Galhad's Bawdy Plans
Fedora Amis

Strangers stared at Elizabeth Bawdin "Bawdy" Carmichael in street clothes. When she wore a black catsuit, swashbuckler boots, and floor-length scarlet cape, people didn't stare. They ogled. Who wouldn't drink in an eyeful of a six-foot-four-inch black Amazon with long knife tied to one leg and painted silver sword banging against the other?

Bawdy walked the three blocks from the St. Louis Convention Center to the Magnolia Hotel. She needed to rest up for a second fencing exhibition that evening. The one she'd just finished left her right arm sore and her left with a painful bruise. *I should've parried that thrust. Good thing Deadpool's épée was made of wood and blunted with a baudry point. I could be on my way to the hospital.*

She passed under the marquee and through the front doors. A few feet inside the lobby, she heard a growl. She didn't stop. Dog, I guess. Didn't know the hotel allows pets. I should have brought my iguana. Add a nice touch to my costume.

"Lady, please stop."

Bawdy paused and looked around, but didn't see anyone. She walked on.

"Tall lady. In case you haven't noticed, I'm still your prisoner. Please stop!"

Bawdy looked down at something her brain couldn't process. A growling dog was gliding across the floor wrapped in the tail of her cloak. Dogs can't talk. She looked around for the owner but saw no one.

"Hel-lo, I'm down here and I'm all twisted up in your cape."

The all-white creature flung aside the tail of Bawdy's cloak to reveal a living thing the size of an Akita. A Japanese dog that speaks English? She blinked several times, then concluded that the whiskered growler was not a dog, but the oddest-looking person she'd ever seen.

He shoved his fox fur coat across the floor and showed Bawdy the problem. His chain mail had hooked the fabric of her mantle.

Bawdy dragged him to a lobby sofa and seated herself to get a better look at the hang up. "So you've been hitching a ride. I thought my cloak was growing heavier by the minute. I should charge you Uber fare."

"I'd gladly pay if you can set me free. In fact, I promise to buy you a drink if you'll loan me a hacksaw."

"How did you get all snarled up, anyway?"

"I hurried to get inside before the door closed. Opening a heavy door is a breeze for you. To me, it's like pushing an elephant through a mail slot."

Bawdy grinned. "I like you. You're funny and you smell like Windex. But how come you latched on to me?"

"I tripped and fell on your train. My metal links got caught in your hem. When I tried to stand, you pulled the rug out from under me—not figuratively speaking. You have no idea how strong you are."

Bawdy worked the chain mail free and adjusted his headdress around his shoulders. "This steel headscarf is too big for you. What are you supposed to be?"

"I'll have you know this is exactly like Big Papa Pump's."

"The wrestler?"

"Yes indeed, the wrestler. I admire big people. Wish I could be one."

"You might not think so if you were one."

"I'd give my mint-in-the-package Starship Enterprise and my William Shatner autographed Captain Kirk to be tall as you."

"Believe me, there are drawbacks."

"Such as?"

"Takes three minutes to stoop down and pick up a dropped penny.

Won't bore you with more."

He stood, slipped into his coat, and bowed. "Mam'selle, I thank you for your most courteous rescue."

"I get it now. You're a wrestler with a gimmick. You play the white knight of King Arthur's round table."

"Close enough. M'lady, would it please you to join me for a libation in yonder taproom?" He bowed again.

"It would please me greatly, kind sir."

With a flourish of his snowy Pinkwhite Chinchilla hat, he directed her towards Robie's bar.

"Since you're a pro, would you mind if I ask you about how to work up a character? What do you call it? Persona. I need a persona. Something to attract attention."

He chuckled. "If you were to attract more attention than you already do, you'd have to fend off the paparazzi with a flame thrower."

"I don't want a swarm of shutterbugs. I do want a new job. Reminds me of another drawback to being big. I have acres more skin for insects to bite than you do—but still only ten fingernails for scratching."

He licked his index finger and drew two imaginary tally marks in the air. "Two for you. I'll be waiting for a third."

"Don't get me started on airplanes and sports cars." She held up three fingers, then four. "Plus, I can think of at least thirty-three more."

"Why thirty-three?"

"The number of my worthless ex-boyfriends."

"On to blithe thoughts of better beaus." He intertwined his fingers. "So, you want to be repeatedly smacked down on four-hundred feet of not-very-soft canvas. And that sounds to you like a dream job. Pray tell, how do you make a living now?"

"Two more drinks and I might give you details. But, enough about me. Tell me about yourself. What's your handle?"

"I'm called Galhad, the politest and purest of all the knights."

"Aren't there three syllables in Galahad?"

"Not the way I use it. Do you truly want to become a professional wrestler?"

"Not really. I want to get a long-running part in a Sci-Fi franchise. Be a superhero or super villain. I'm not choosy."

"You epitomize the guise of gargantuan greatness."

She picked him up by his armpits and hoisted him onto a barstool. She did not ask permission. "I can't decide which way to go. A word meister such as you could be a great help. Should I wear a headdress of animated rubber snakes and call myself the Medusa of Mendocino?"

"You're from California, too."

"Beautiful Pacoima, home of "La Bamba" Richie Valens and earthquakes. Would you please focus on my problem? Maybe I ought to try for something funny." She flung both arms toward the ceiling. "Let me introduce the Sheep-Dip Queen and Fencing Champion of Brooklyn."

Galhad laughed. Against his pale skin and chalk-white whiskers, his blue eyeballs sparkled like two iridescent marbles in a saucer of milk. "Quite droll, Mam'selle."

"Brooklyn isn't funny enough. How about Winnetka?" She scrunched up her face. "Let me introduce the Sheep-Dip Queen and Fencing Champion of Winnetka. No. That's not it either. What do you suggest?"

"Hackensack."

"I like it. The Sheep-Dip Queen and Fencing Champion of Hackensack. Is that Hackensack, Minnesota or Hackensack, New Jersey?"

"New Jersey, if you can master the accent."

"Wat would it cawst me to troiy?"

"Not bad." He turned to the bartender and announced, "My I present The Sheep-Dip Queen and Fencing Champion of Hackensack? The beautiful villainess of that brand-new science fiction thriller— Vampire Women in the Avocado Jungle of Toast."

"Perfect. Wait. Wait. I make an even better villain when I wear these." She touched various parts of her anatomy, darted glances around the bar, and slipped off the stool. She checked under the stool, then leaned forward to look over the bar. "Thought it might have fallen on the floor."

"Something missing?"

"My tote bag. I have a custom-made set of vampire fangs. They make me look mega-ferocious and mega-sexy. I must have left the bag on the couch in the lobby."

"I'll help you look for it." Galhad turned to slide down from the stool but need not have bothered.

Bawdy picked him up and set him on the floor as if she'd been making his life easier for at least a decade or two. She reached to take his hand as if he were a child but thought better of it. The pair made an even more unlikely couple in motion than sitting still. She took big strides while he trotted to keep up.

When she saw no sign of her bag, Bawdy started to bend down. Galhad said, "Allow me, m'lady. Looking under a sofa is the one thing I can do better than you. I'm closer to the floor."

She cruised out the front door to search up and down Eighth Street, then returned with a hangdog look.

In her absence, he'd hustled around the lobby chairs and tables. "Not in the lobby. Did you find it?"

She shook her head. "Either I lost it at Comicon, or someone stole it."

"May I escort you to the convention center to check with lost and found?"

"No big loss. A few pesos." Bawdy patted her bosom. "I keep my I.D. and credit cards close to my heart. Still, I'll miss it. A gift from my ex. I like to spit on it from time to time."

They returned to the bar. He said, "It'll turn up. Hateful reminders always do."

She changed the subject. "Guess I know why you came here. You're a Trekkie. Did Shatner autograph your doll?"

"We collectors call them 'action figures.' And yes, I paid fifty bucks to the original Captain Kirk of the USS Enterprise. Well worth it."

She sighed. "I'd like to sit in autograph row with the big stars. I'd even sign for free."

This time, he changed the subject. "What drew you to St. Louis Fan Expo 2022?"

"I heard a rumor that Bill Condon might come."

"No doubt I should know who Bill Condon is but..." He raised his eyebrows.

"Condon directed the last two Twilight films. A TV series is in the works. Who else would they get? I mean he's a screenwriter, producer, director—the whole ball of dough. I was hoping he'd be a speaker in one of the sessions and maybe I could catch his eye."

"If any man decided to throw his eyeballs around, I bet he'd make sure you have a catcher's mitt."

"A pun. You're clever, and cute, too." Bawdy pulled at her earlobe. "It was just a rumor. He's not in town. Guess I'll have to make do with Michael Rooker."

"From Guardians of the Galaxy. Not a good guy but not a total villain. Is his character's ambivalence why you find him attractive?"

"Not really. I like him because he's blue. You admire big people. I admire people of color. We brighten the world." She smoothed her hair with a graceful hand.

"Look at you. Making a pun. We seem to have at least one thing in common."

A voice came from the entrance to the bar. "There's an odd couple Neil Simon never thought of. Big black freak and little white freak. What kind of geek show do you two do?"

When Bawdy scowled, Galhad said, "Don't look at him. He'll go away."

"I know the hotel allows dogs, but Babe, this is too much. What is the white furball, anyway? A Baby Bigfoot?"

When Bawdy started to turn, Galhad took hold of her arm. "Don't do what bullies goad you to do. I've learned from bitter experience."

"Big Babe, turn around so I can see you. If you look as good from the front as you do from the back, I'll buy you a drink. The yeti, too."

She removed Galhad's hand from her arm. He shook his head. "Better to wait him out. Obnoxious people have weak minds and short attention spans."

"I've had enough." Bawdy pushed away from the bar and turned to face the mouthy creep. "Well, if it isn't the freakiest freak of the Wizard World freakfest."

"At your service, Babe." The tormentor turned out to be a gigantic fellow with even more shaggy hair than Galhad. None other than an amateur version of the Star Wars favorite, Chewbacca the Wookie. This one didn't speak in the whiny growl of Wookie lingo. Nor did he wear a proper mask—just a fright wig and tufts of facial hair. Most impressive were his eyebrows which looked like two-pound woolly worms.

With a hand to his head, Bawdy spun Galhad around. "The mean old bugbear turned out to be an oversized teddy bear. But this one is about as cuddly as an armful of electric eels."

Chewy shuffled to the bar and offered to bump paws. "May I join you and your pet polar bear?"

Bawdy refused the fist bump.

Galhad looked at his pocket watch. "We were just finishing our drinks. We don't want to miss our Arch time, do we, Bawdy?"

Bawdy tried to keep surprise from showing on her face. "The Arch—of course—I nearly forgot. We'd better get a move on." She ducked down to whisper in Galhad's ear. "Did you really reserve a tram time at the Arch?"

"Put on plastic yesterday. I ordered transportation, too." He paid the bar bill, took Bawdy's hand, and led her to the hotel garage. Chewy shuffled along behind.

Bawdy beamed all the way. A limo. How grand. But no sleek stretch Lincoln awaited. Nor was there a gleaming Cadillac sedan. Not even a Mini Cooper or a Vespa. The proposed transportation was an electric

Segway. She traded the attendant her sword and knife for a helmet.

Chewy said, "There's only one of those things."

Bawdy took Galhad's hands and lifted him smoothly onto her shoulders. "We only need one."

"Mind if I tag along? It's not far."

Both heads turned and looked at him but said nothing.

When an Amazon, a Wookie, and a white bundle of fur segway down a sidewalk, people get out of the way.

Chewy hollered, "Hey, gorgeous Babe. Are you two a team? Do you have some kind of weird circus act? If you don't, I have a suggestion. A magic act where you make him disappear. I'd pay to see that."

Galhad piped up, "I met this lovely lady quite recently, but I hope we might find mutual benefit in our acquaintance."

"Mighty big words for such a little fart."

Bawdy snapped at Chewy. "All the farting around here is coming out of your asshole mouth."

"Sorry, Babe, didn't mean to offend. I'm just curious. Here's my question for the little scoop of white rice. Did some mean old bad guy dunk you in a vat of glue and toss you in a barrel of cotton balls?"

"Will somebody get this big walking carpet out of my way?" Bawdy stuck her chin in the air. "I always wanted to use that line. Makes me feel like Princess Leia."

Chewy ignored her riposte in favor of insulting Galhad again. "Hey little guy, what do you want to be when you grow up? An albino Santa Claus?" When he received no reply from anyone, he said, "Oreo cookie center? Maybe a bleached blond Ewok."

Even wait-'em-out Galhad bristled at that. "I proudly say I played an Ewok in two feature films and both TV movies. I'm memorialized on film as a Star Wars character. Something I doubt you could ever achieve."

"My, my. Were you also immortalized as an original munchkin in the Wizard of Oz?"

"I'd have to be a hundred years old."

"You look it."

Bawdy leaned forward on the Segway to leave Chewy behind. Maybe that would shut him up.

Fifteen minutes later, the Segway reached the Arch. Bawdy set Galhad on the pavement.

"What a thrill when you speeded up to lose that Chewbacca pest."

"Glad you enjoyed the ride."

"Wonderful. For the first time in my life, everybody looked up to me. I've never been so tall."

"It was our best chance to ditch the Wookie. Still, I'm afraid he'll follow us. Let's hustle on up in the Arch. If you really have tickets, that is."

"I do. Do you know why I wanted to go to the top? I'd be taller than anybody in the whole city—except for the people also at the top. How many could there be? Twenty or so, I guess."

"Look behind us. Have you ever seen a more determined shag rug?" Bawdy pointed toward a loping Wookie whose bandolier flopped with every stride.

Chewy panted as he came to a stop. "You can't dump me that easy. We used to be close and cozy."

"I'd rather get cozy with prickly pear cacti. Higher I.Q. and better personal hygiene. Can't you tell you're not wanted?"

"I can tell, Babe. I'm just not ready to give up. Not until I say what I have to say."

"Seems to me you already said too much. But go on. I'll give you thirty seconds."

"It's just not right. A beautiful girl with a pipsqueak freak. You belong with someone your own size. Me, for example."

"You could grow ten feet straight up and still never be tall enough to tie Galhad's shoes. He's a person with feelings, who deserves as much respect as every other human being. Something you might understand if you ever manage to become one." Bawdy and Galhad left Chewy rummaging in his utility belt, opening zippers, and poking around the contents.

Bawdy pursed her lips and crooned, "Poor big baby. One woolly-worm eyebrow fell off."

Galhad said, "I carry spirit gum to stick on my whiskers. Should I make him a peace offering?"

"No need. He just found a stick of Wrigley's Juicy Fruit gum."

An hour later, Bawdy and Galhad gazed out the windows from the top of the Gateway Arch. Both oohed and aahed at the Mississippi sparkling in the late afternoon sun.

Galhad said, "I want to set the record straight—be entirely truthful."

"You don't have to. I trust you."

"You shouldn't. I let you believe I'm a professional wrestler. I'm not. I'm an actor just like you."

"I know that. You played an Ewok. That's great. When the call comes out for actors in the Twilight TV series, maybe we could audition together. I'd be a ravishing vampire, pun intended. You'd be spectacular as a white werewolf."

"Even if we don't get the parts, they'll never forget us." Galhad paused. "There's more. I tangled myself in your cloak on purpose, and I stole your tote bag so I could meet you."

"What?"

"This is as good a time as any to apologize and tell you how grateful I am for these two hours. I'll cherish them forever." He looked up at her with a tear rolling down one cheek. "I hid your bag under a sofa in the lobby lounge. I'll get it for you when we return. I'll pay for anything that might be missing. You probably don't want to be seen with me anymore. I'll take a taxi to the hotel when we leave."

Bawdy smiled. "That's just silly. I don't need anything from the bag but my vampire fangs. Even that's not a problem. I could have new ones made."

Galhad brushed away the tear. "So, you don't hate me?"

"Never could. Now would be a good time to make more confessions. But please, let me go first. It's true that I'm an actress, but that doesn't pay my bills. Pole dancing does. Also, the big jerk dressed up as

Chewbacca is my most recent ex. Yes, he gave me the tote bag I spit on when I need to tamp down the rage I feel whenever I think about him."

"I can't blame him for following you around. The moment I saw you, I fell faster than a mudslide in Topanga Canyon. You're the most beautiful woman I've ever seen. I'm even besmitten enough to think you might grow to like me or, if heaven smiles, regard me as something more than a friend."

"You want to date me?"

"More than you can imagine."

"I suppose that's not entirely out of the question. You're a big improvement over a thousand creeps I dated just because they were basketball players. Is that the last of the confessions?"

"Just one more. Well, two, actually."

"Shoot."

Galhad took a deep breath. "You know the Gal in Galhad. That's what I am. A gal. I'm a woman—and I like women. I especially like you."

Bawdy did a double take. Well, isn't that a kick in the assumptions? I don't know whether to kiss that face or smack it into next Tuesday. She pondered for a count of ten. Don't be too hasty in rejecting Galhad. He-she's had too much of that. We both have.

"Aren't you going to say something?"

"You've been a man for a couple of hours but a woman for less than a minute. I need time to think." She'd never been interested in lesbianism. Still heterosexualism hasn't done her any favors. And he-she is terminally adorable. "You have a deep voice for a woman especially one who is..."

"We used to be midgets. Now we're little people. Just like anyone else, but we can sleep in a doghouse or hide in a golf bag."

"Just a little bundle of wisecracks and wisdom." Bawdy took Gal's hands and smoothly lifted the little amiga to her shoulders. "We'll work out all the other stuff but for now, one wish has come true. You're taller than everyone else in the whole city of St. Louis."

Go West
JD Frain

Feeling the twinge in her back when she bent over, Dottie van der Weiss finally acknowledged this job demanded more than she could physically give. She straightened to her full height on artificial knees and slumped into a chair to consider her deadline. Her husband wouldn't stay gone forever, even if she prayed the rosary and changed the locks.

Walter van der Weiss had made his choices—usually young and blonde—and Dottie made her own choice: time to move on. He didn't care how he'd hurt her pride, so she decided she'd inflict a little pain of her own in the only place Walter could feel it—his pocketbook. She needed an influx of cash to jumpstart her new life, and she knew how to make a withdrawal.

Upstairs in her townhome, she took one more look inside the guest room. Pondered one more time her ability to accomplish this task. Then she rubbed her back and shook her head, knowing she couldn't do this on her own. It was hard to admit she needed help. Unlike the Monday crossword puzzle which was always easy. She loved her routine so much, she forgot about her deadline for a moment. Was she procrastinating, or letting her plan percolate?

She walked downstairs to the kitchen and prepared eggs and toast for breakfast. Poured a cup of coffee. Opened the newspaper to the daily crossword. She smiled at 17 Across, a clue she'd seen other days and an omen for this day: Arch-itect Saarinen. She looked out the window at the south leg of the Gateway Arch, stainless steel gleaming in the sunlight, and wrote EERO in the boxes. By 10 a.m., she had traded procrastinating for planning.

She started by making a list of the people who could help. Names she'd learned from Walter's so-called business. It was a short list. She could reach them by phone.

* * *

Amber was in the middle of snorting a line of cocaine, calculating how she was going to pay the electric bill before the utility company cut her off, when the landline she shared with her mother rang. She always paid her phone bill. Her mother was out, so answering the call fell to Amber. Her mother would be out for six to ten years, according to the state. Twenty-eight years old and Amber was finally living on her own. Without moving out of her house.

"This is Amber," she said, then sniffed like someone who had just taken a line of coke.

"Oh dear," a woman's voice said. "I was looking for Candace."

"My mother," Amber said. "She's out. On vacation."

"When do you expect her back?"

"It might be a while," Amber eyed the remaining line of coke on the table.

"Oh, I see."

"I'm helping while she's gone. You need something?"

Then the call got more interesting.

"This is Dottie van der Weiss," the caller said. "Candace was going to help us with a fizzbo this weekend."

"A fizz—what?"

"Sorry. FSBO. For Sale by Owner. Walter and I are selling our townhome, and Candace was going to play hostess for potential buyers on Sunday. Perhaps, if you have the time…"

Amber grinned like her Powerball numbers had just flashed on the screen. She recognized Walter van der Weiss's name, knew about his townhouse in downtown St. Louis, and so she turned up her charm.

"I'm your girl, Dottie."

"You'll be perfect for the role. I'd do it myself, but I just can't sit still and watch people go through my things. And my husband, well, Walter can't sit still, plain and simple."

"It's right up my alley," Amber said. She could no more sell a townhouse than build one, but this was once-in-a-lifetime stuff in her world, and she knew how to seize an opportunity. Besides, she wouldn't have to sell the house; she just had to get inside for a short time. She wouldn't even need a weapon to pull this off. That was the kicker that would impress Mom, sent to Vandalia to serve her sentence for aggravated robbery. Mom, who foolishly brought a gun to her last job "for my own protection," would have to tip her cap to Amber this time.

Walter van der Weiss had been on Mom's radar for years, and Amber wasn't opposed to cashing in on leftovers. If she pulled off a heist at Walter's townhouse, Amber would become a millionaire before Mom started breathing free air. The look on Mom's face would be worth half a million alone.

* * *

Amber had six days to prepare, a lifetime when you could use the internet to study everything you needed to pretend you knew. Sunday arrived with a cloudless sky, and the sun kissed Amber on the cheek. She was about to claim her million-dollar reward, so she dressed for the occasion. Her shortest pink skirt, paired with a mismatched blue blazer, and turquoise boots purloined from Goodwill. She considered blue lipstick to pull the ensemble together but couldn't find any. After a couple of hard years, she could probably use a splash of paint, but otherwise she was move-in ready.

Amber stood on the sidewalk at the entrance to Gateway Townhomes, 630 South Broadway. A stone archway, modeled to replicate the Gateway Arch, stood for tenants to walk under before entering the building. Amber worked up a smile and whispered, "Just be the incredible person you are." The affirmation was unconvincing, but she passed beneath the arch anyway.

In the kitchen, Dottie van der Weiss balanced a beehive hairdo and peered over the top of horn-rimmed glasses. She wore a muumuu dress and crumbs from a recent bag of Doritos. With a finger to her chin, she assessed Amber's appearance and, with zero subtlety, scrunched her lips and shook her head.

"Well, anyway," Dottie said, "I'm on my way out. Two hours, you say?"

Where was Walter? Amber's eyes darted around the room. She wanted to know the location of all her enemies.

"Sometimes an open house will last more than two hours. If we get lucky—well, not lucky so much as, what's the word…"

"Just don't get lucky in the bedroom please," Dottie said, a shiver to show her displeasure in case Amber hadn't picked up on it.

"Heavens no," Amber said. "I meant someone might return at the end with an offer."

"If you say so, hon."

Amber caught herself admiring a couple of paintings before snapping her head and resuming her important search. Paintings were so hard to move and so easy to sell to an undercover cop. "Where is Wal—Mr. van der Weiss?"

"The address, dear," Dottie ignored her. "You know the significance, right?"

"Yes, 630 South Broadway."

"Your attention to accuracy is commendable. I can see you've arrived at the correct address. But do you understand the significance of the street number? So you can pass along the fun fact to buyers."

Amber had no idea what Dottie was talking about, but that had never stopped her. She switched on her smile, probably due for a remodel, but perfectly serviceable. "Of course. I'll save the explanation for our best prospects. And is Walter—"

"Try to keep up, dear." Dottie was halfway down the hallway toward the front door. Amber hurried after her, down the front steps and out to the street where a cab idled. Dottie coerced her frame plus what

Amber-the-Realtor might describe as a bump-out addition into the back seat of the taxi.

"Don't let anyone run the faucet too long, dear."

Amber eased the cab door shut, resisting the temptation to dent Dottie. "No need to worry, Mrs. Van der Weiss." Amber waved.

The window lowered. "They won't sit on my toilet, will they?"

Amber maintained her smile, her face displaying the first signs of lockjaw. "The toilet will be included in your sale, so think of it like an Airbnb rental."

"Oh dear," Dottie said as Amber backed away and almost tripped on the curb. "They can look at it, but they don't need to touch it. Or flush it, good heavens."

Amber leaned toward the driver's door and encouraged him with another wave. "Thank you. Drive careful."

The man didn't move.

Amber tapped her palm on the car roof. "Okay, then."

The cabbie stared straight ahead. "No one told me where we're going."

Amber raised her eyebrows.

Dottie chimed in. "Missouri Botanical Gardens on Shaw."

The tires didn't screech, but the cab finally rolled away.

To exhaust fumes, Amber called, "Don't hurry back." A glance at her watch showed ten minutes until the open house—might be enough time. She rushed through the archway and hurried up the sidewalk, as much as a rookie in high-heeled boots could pull off the trick. She shoved open the door and froze.

"I'm sorry," a woman said, "we were a few minutes early, so we thought we'd see if the house was already open." Then, as if pre-empting the accusation, "The door was unlocked."

"Well, come in," Amber said to the couple who had translated the Welcome mat too literally. They signed a sheet on the dining room table and strolled through the property. Before they left, an elderly couple waltzed in and before they left a woman came through and before long the open house would close without a free moment for Amber. A successful event for most realtors. An afternoon of agony for Amber.

Ten minutes before closing, a woman called from the back.

"The garden here? Would we need to take care of it or is there a gardener?"

This one probably expected a cook came with the kitchen. Amber winced as she offered her picket-fence smile, the opening to every answer. "You're free to hire a gardener. But the land here? It's the back yard to the townhome."

"Yard, huh? That what they call it?"

Amber could not disagree with her assessment about the postage-stamp-sized yard, and then she laughed at the irony of that thought. Maybe Walter planned it that way!

"You'll find it surprisingly relaxing out here," Amber said, and the words surprised her as they spilled out. Maybe she should consider a career in real estate. What do they earn, six percent and falling? Commission in her current job was one hundred percent and she didn't have to work most Sundays. She waved off the idea. Merely considering it was tiresome.

"I'm not sure I will." Together, they pretended to admire the so-called yard. Or maybe this woman simply appreciated the smell of yeast wafting down on a soft breeze from the Anheuser-Busch brewery.

"Do you live nearby?" Amber asked, uncomfortable with the silence.

"West." A horn honked to drown out her answer, but Amber plunged on without the detail.

"Oh, then you'll love it here," she said, not sure where that conclusion came from, but having nothing else in her realtor's toolkit. She wasn't sure which direction west was from where they stood. Embarrassed, she called upon her reliable smile before retreating to the dining room. The woman, final client of the day, left quietly a few moments later, open house now closed.

Business time at last! Amber locked the front door, removed her boots with a thankful sigh, dug her toes into the thick carpet, and raced upstairs. Halfway up, the doorbell rang.

She waited. Five seconds. Late arrivals? They'd missed out.

If it didn't ring again, she'd continue into the master bedroom and begin her search. Five more seconds. She climbed the final steps to the second floor when the front door squeaked open. Had she locked it wrong? So sorry, we're closed, set an appointment for tomorrow if it's still on the market. She inched down three steps and craned her neck for a view of the interloper.

"Amber, dear," Dottie called. "You locked me out. I was almost to the door when I saw you close it."

"Dottie!" Amber rushed down the stairs. "You're back already?"

"The Garden is hosting a music festival. Heathens stamping around, probably killing the plants. Did you get time to relax here, look around at all?"

"Busy from the word go. I didn't—"

"No downtime? Shame." Dottie sounded oddly disappointed at her busy open house.

"Several people showed interest." Amber needed Dottie out of the house, if just for a short time. She seized an idea. Mom would be so proud. "In fact, one couple is returning—"

"Okay, okay. I need to get my green hat. I forgot I'm meeting Walter for early dinner."

"Darling hat. I saw it upstairs," Amber said. "I'll fetch it."

"Oh, you're a dear."

Amber rushed upstairs and into the master bedroom. Plucking the hat, she spun around and caught movement in her peripheral vision. Wedged behind the door stood six-foot, two inches of a man. Early thirties, wavy dark hair with a scruffy beard, and wearing a windbreaker, he offered a supplicating smile.

"Going by Amber now, are we?"

Her chin dropped. She knew all six-foot, two inches of D.J. Tucker. He was a fixer-upper, but he had a desirable neighborhood beneath his

Levi's that she'd happily visited on a couple of occasions. If it were possible to yell a whisper, Amber did. "What the hell are you doing here?"

"Same as you, I suspect. Clever outfit, but the green hat isn't a match."

She brushed off his fashion advice. "How did you even find this place?"

"The master bedroom? It was the room with the bed, love. The guestroom only has bookcases. Pray we don't have to search through those." Old charm in his cheeky grin, lots of potential in his raised eyebrows.

"I didn't see you come in."

"You were talking to a woman about the the back yard if she got the script right."

"She had zero curb appeal, that one."

"No, I don't suppose you'd find her aesthetically pleasing. Where shall we begin our search, uh, Amber, is it?"

She straightened in her best attempt to show off the breathtaking views of her realtor outfit. "I don't know your plan, but I'm here to sell a house."

"Certainly, love. And to add the Inverted Jenny to your sales commission?"

To a commoner, the Inverted Jenny represented 24-cent postage. To a philatelist, the rare 1918 stamp meant a treasure as lustrous as gold. To a thief, a single stamp translated into a potential for a quarter-million dollars.

Walter van der Weiss owned four.

"How do you know about the Jenny?" Amber asked.

"We run in the same crowd, snookums. Thought I'd meet your mother here."

"She moved. Lives in a gated community now."

"Oh, big house, right. Well, back to the present. Everyone cleared out? Open house closed now?"

Amber could send D.J. out to encounter Dottie, but that would raise suspicions. She could call Dottie upstairs and they could catch D.J. together, but no telling how either would react. Dottie might call Walter home from dinner, crushing Amber's plans like a failed home inspection.

D.J. came out from behind the door. "While you're thinking, I'll start searching. Finders keepers." He walked across the room to a closet door and reached for the knob.

"Amber?" Dottie called from the stairway. "Have you found my hat?"

D.J. jumped. Thankfully, the carpet muffled his landing. "She's still here?" He opened the closet to step inside, but it wasn't a closet. It was the bathroom.

Amber scurried after him. "Don't say a word."

D.J. winked. "Here's to a wee bit more time, eh?" He flushed the toilet.

In the hallway, Dottie squealed, "Oh, my, so sorry." Her footsteps disappeared down the stairway.

"I could tell her about you," Amber said, jabbing a finger into D.J.

"I could tell her about you," he answered. "Realtor with a rap sheet. Jolly good."

"Are you carrying?" She knew D.J.'s abhorrence for guns, but she had to confirm what she was up against.

He raised his hands and wiggled his fingers. "These are the only weapons I need. Too bad your mother didn't follow my advice."

She bit her lower lip and clutched the green hat. "Leave my mom out of this. Okay, we'll cut a deal. There's no way just one of us walks out of here with the Jenny."

"Four Jennies," he corrected, "but I'm sure you already knew."

Damn him. She'd have to split this commission with D.J. "Dottie is leaving to meet Walter. I'll get rid of her."

"I'll wait here for you, darling."

Amber growled, more lion than kitten. "I'm not your darling."

"I'm never quite sure what to call you. It's Amber today, right?"

She hustled downstairs with the green hat.

"You're too kind," Dottie said. "I hope it isn't inconvenient to take me to Walter. Can you spare a few minutes?"

Amber stumbled for an excuse. "I was going to stay so—"

"Take me first. Come back to meet the buyers, dear."

"I'll book you an—"

"I'm not riding in one of those Ubers you kids like. Taking a ride from some random stranger."

"Isn't that what a cab is?"

"Thank you. Let's hurry along, I can't keep Walter waiting." Dottie stepped through the doorway, Amber in tow. McGurk's Irish Pub was five minutes away in Soulard. In the car, Amber offered the details she could remember regarding the open house and embellished the rest. Dottie responded with "Oh" or "I see" where appropriate.

"You told them about the address, right?" Dottie said.

If they showed up, they knew the address. Amber should have asked one of the visitors about the significance of the address. Six thirty. Who was born June thirtieth? Maybe it was a horoscope thing. Was that Cancer?

"Didn't have to," Amber lied. "Everyone knew."

"They knew the significance of six thirty?"

Saying it like that made it sound like a clock. Was something hidden in the clock? "Yes, they did," she lied again.

"That the Gateway Arch is six-hundred-thirty feet tall and six-hundred-thirty feet wide?"

"What the—that can't be true."

"I thought you said they all knew."

"Is it an optical illusion?"

"The irony should be worth an extra thousand on the sales price if you sell it right."

Amber tried to get her mind back in the game. "It's a nice place, no matter the address."

* * *

Dottie had narrowed Walter's hiding place to two locations inside the townhouse. She couldn't give any more attention to the bathroom, her second choice. She needed Amber to focus on the most likely location. That's why she'd left a clock unplugged and set for six-thirty in the guest room, but that hint seemed lost on Amber. She'd need to think of a more obvious clue, and she only had a couple of minutes to do it.

"Was it warm enough, dear? Did anyone complain about the heat?"

Amber looked disinterested. "Oh, there were complaints, Dottie. The back yard is the size of a post—it's super small. The vanity in the master bath only has one sink. People whine about everything, right?"

"But not about the heat?"

"One lady complained while looking out the bedroom window. She thought the Arch spanned the Mississippi river. Like that's your fault, right?"

Hints were wasted with Amber. "The stairs are a burden," Dottie said. "But the guestroom radiator is the worst. It's never worked. Never been hot. Walter says he likes the style." She rolled her eyes. "I think the best thing to do would be to get rid of it."

* * *

Dottie got out at the curb in front of McGurk's. Amber didn't stay to watch her enter the restaurant. Instead, she gathered enough will to ease down on the accelerator instead of punching it to the floor. Walter and Dottie should take ninety minutes or so before returning. Unless Dottie started yapping about the open house. Walter wouldn't take kindly to missing a meal, but he'd miss his stamps even more. Walter would rush home. Amber still wondered why Walter hadn't shown his face in the first place, but she wouldn't use the full ninety minutes and risk him surprising her. She needed to get in and out as quickly as possible.

D.J. was upstairs in the guest bathroom when Amber returned.

"Any luck?" she asked.

"I'm fitting this safe back in the floor. Picked the lock and thought we were in, but nothing here except worthless old coins."

"A safe in the bathroom?" Amber was suspicious. D.J. was as trustworthy as a FSBO with no inspection.

"I found it a little fishy, too," D.J. said, "but it turned out to be a red herring."

"Was the combination six-three-zero?"

"I don't know. I just listened for the tumblers to click."

He moved a hamper over the fake tile in the floor of the bathroom closet. "Checked all the usual places. We may have to search the book collection, love. Probably a hollow book in there somewhere. Under which title might one hide a million dollars of Inverted Jennies? Does our friend Walter own any novels by Terence Stamp?"

"He's an actor, D.J. Nice try."

"Walter's an actor? Thought he made his money—"

"What's in your pockets?" Amber didn't believe him. A hidden bathroom safe was a potential place for valuable stamps.

"Sorry, love. Nothing in my pockets. I was just happy to see you as the saying goes." He turned his jeans pockets inside out.

"What about the radiator?"

"Sorry?"

"In the guestroom."

"Big fella. What about it?"

"They don't have radiant heat."

"Then why—oh. You're clever when you're Amber."

She didn't tell him Dottie had unwittingly slipped her a hint. They rushed to the guest bedroom, squeezing through the doorway together. The radiator was solid and sturdy. D.J. squatted, clasped his hands underneath the nest of metal pipes and let out a grunt to make an Olympic weightlifter proud. He muscled the radiator inch by grueling inch into a new spot on the floor. Amber spied the misplaced carpet that covered a small floorboard.

Using the same tool he'd employed with the bathroom tile, D.J. pried open the floorboard. Compared to moving the radiator, removing the floorboard came easy. Amber pulled out a small album the size of a passport. She opened it and let out a gasp. Four Inverted Jennies inside a plastic sheet. One voluptuous vertical row. She slipped the plastic pouch between two pieces of cardboard and placed it in her pocket.

"Looks like decision time, love," D.J. said. "How to divvy our winnings."

"Easy." Amber tapped her pocket. "I'll fence them, and we'll split the take."

"Spoken with a straight face, doll. Perhaps you'll manage my retirement portfolio too."

"What do you suggest? We can't break them apart. The value plummets."

"Planning to add them to our stamp collection, are we? Of course, we can break them apart. And we will."

"Okay, you win. We don't have much time."

"But we have enough time to split them here."

"Walter could walk in the door any minute, and I don't plan to be here when that happens. We'll cut them. Each of us takes two stamps."

"But there are three of us."

"Three?"

"Yes," D.J. said. "Rosa, your friend from the back yard, is waiting a block away. She won't be satisfied with a twenty-five percent take if you get fifty."

"She's your problem, D.J. We're not tearing a stamp into thirds. Besides, you got a bonus while I drove the old bag to meet Walter. Nothing but worthless coins in that bathroom safe? Please."

"Okay," D.J. reconsidered. "Two stamps each."

Amber used the cardboard to carefully separate the stamps. "Now let's get out of here." They replaced the carpet, slid the radiator into place, and scurried downstairs. D.J. pulled open the townhouse's front door to flee.

Amber saw her first. "Dottie!" Quickly put on her realtor smile.

* * *

"Lovely home," a tall, bearded man in a windbreaker said. "Are you thinking of buying?"

Dottie didn't move. Didn't speak. Looked them over from head to toe.

"This is D. J., the gentleman who came back for a second viewing, Dottie. I was telling you."

The man smiled. "You may have to outbid me, princess, if you're looking to buy this beauty." He turned to Amber. "Thanks again. I'll be in touch."

Dottie shifted her Cape Cod frame in the doorway. "Oh my, a strong man is hard to find. Might I borrow you in the kitchen, dear? Just take a moment."

He hesitated. "Well, actually I was—"

"Absolutely he can help," Amber said, her eyes searching behind Dottie, likely looking for Walter to arrive.

"Kitchen's straight in the back," Dottie said, "in case you'd forgotten." She herded Amber and her friend toward the back.

"Indeed. Lovely kitchen," he said. "Modern, yet … well, modern is enough."

Amber scowled. "What happened to dinner with Walter?"

Dottie ignored her, which she found pleasurable. In the kitchen, she said, "I need to move the fridge. Does anyone have a gun?"

"A gun!" Amber blurted, laughing at the absurdity of the question.

"Heavens, I never carry one," D.J. said. "They scare me."

"Boo." Dottie pulled her hand from the pocket of her muumuu and raised a Beretta Bobcat.

"Dottie!" Amber jumped back.

"Oh, dear," Dottie said. "I found that rather fun."

D. J. raised his arms. "That's enough fun for—"

"I'll do the talking from here on, if you please." Dottie, impatient, swung the Beretta toward him.

He straightened and nodded.

"Can I trust you've found the Inverted Jennies? Took a little longer than I expected. I was getting bored waiting out front. Between the radiator and the bathroom, I thought my clues gave a perfect hint, Amber. And the clock on the wall above the guest room radiator. I expected better."

Amber rolled her eyes. "A broken clock for a clue? Get real. How did you pick me anyway?"

"I didn't. I called your mother who would have probably figured out the clues, but you answered the phone. During the call, you fell in love with the idea of robbing us. Well, robbing Walter, he's the collector. Your enthusiasm came across as loud as your outfit. So, I chose you to host the Open House. I didn't invite your boyfriend though."

"I didn't either," Amber protested.

Dottie pulled out a pair of handcuffs and directed Amber to put one cuff around her wrist and loop the other end through the handle on the refrigerator door.

"Your turn, young man. Sorry I didn't catch your name, or is it just DJ?" He put the open cuff over his wrist without volunteering his name.

"Now then, if you'll set the Jennies on the counter here, we'll all live happily ever after."

"Alas, I'm afraid we never found them, love," D. J. said, using his most sincere voice.

Dottie fired once at his foot, and the bullet ricocheted off the tile floor. One scream later, he pulled the stamps from his inside jacket pocket. A diamond bracelet fell out at the same time.

"You wouldn't be leaving if you hadn't found them. It was the radiator, right? I knew Walter wouldn't trust them in the bathroom even if they were in a safe. Thank you for moving that monster radiator. Lord knows I tried, but I'm not so young anymore."

Dottie shifted the Beretta. Amber wasted no time putting her stamps on the counter. She looked once more toward the front door.

"Walter's not coming, dear," Dottie said, reading Amber's mind. "Nassau for two more days, maybe three. If he gets on a roll at the craps table, he'll stay another week. He lost this bet though. Gambled on leaving me for a younger woman."

D. J. tried a last gasp, mixed with a bit of flattery. "Sweetheart, let's go find him and give the scalawag a message."

Dottie shook her head. "I'll go west, young man. Even beyond Greeley, Colorado. Somewhere farther west that never needs radiant heat. And when I get there, I'll send a note thanking each of you." She winked and held up the Inverted Jennies. "I've got stamps for your postcards."

Mann for the Job
Laurence Lovan

Mike Hammer, Peter Gunn, Phillip Marlowe… I wondered if they ever snuck around seedy motels with a Polaroid trying to get photos of hubby with his secretary, next door neighbor, or whomever. Smile, you're on Candid Camera, a-hole. Probably not. They always had hot babes show up with problems only they could solve. They also had heads of iron that couldn't be dented no matter how many times they were clubbed from behind.

You'd think with a name like Kevin Mann, private investigator, I could score some nooky too. I'd had business cards made up. Kevin Mann, the Man for the Job. Okay, I'll admit, that's lame. But hey, Allan Pinkerton built a detective empire out of an eyeball and the logo "We Never Sleep". Talk about lame.

It was thoughts like this that were keeping me occupied on this early fall afternoon. I'd parked myself on a small bench where I could see the Gateway Arch in the distance. It was the same bench I'd sat on a few years back and watched as they installed the final piece of the giant horseshoe. It was the same day I'd been let go from the St. Louis Police Department. I hadn't worked a shift in weeks due to time off to recover from a gunshot wound. Which gave them the perfect excuse to release me with a fifty percent disability pension. They tend to frown on rookie patrolmen who rat out fellow officers, embarrass the department. Especially when those fellow officers end up getting ten to twenty in the state pen.

It was evening rush hour, and the handful of war protestors were catching a lot of grief from drivers. Mostly the bird or, "Go back to Russia you effing Commie pinkos." St. Louis wasn't exactly a hotbed of political action. The protestors were doing their best, waving signs and yelling, "Stop the war now!" Most of them were college age, kids dressed in tie-dye, bell bottoms and sandals. One guy claimed to be a Vietnam vet. He wore a fatigue shirt with the sleeves cut off, a peace sign drawn on the back with the logo 'Vietnam Vet', and a pair of ratty jeans. He'd tied a red bandana around his forehead and long stringy hair. He had a bushy Fu Manchu moustache, too.

More vets showed up among the college kids as the war dragged on. A couple of guys from my high school graduating class had been killed in Nam. Another guy I knew had come home physically unwounded but pretty much of an addict with a thousand-yard stare. The fifty percent disability from the SLPD had kept me out of the draft. I was damaged goods.

One of the chicks who looked half stoned, came over with a bucket, panhandling. I gave her a couple of bucks. "Thanks, man," she said and wandered away. A patrolman would be along soon to move them on. Me too, as my attire was similar to the peaceniks. Worn and faded blue bells with white pinstripes, boots, and a black Rolling Stones T-shirt, the one with a gaping mouth and a large red tongue hanging out. My shoulder-length hair matched the hippies but had been washed more recently.

Cops hated protestors and hippies both.

I needed to get going soon anyway. I'd landed a job that didn't include seedy hotels... I hoped. A pair of senior citizens had hired me to locate their missing nineteen-year-old granddaughter, Ruth. They'd looked askance at me at first, but I was able to convince them my appearance allowed me to fit in perfectly with the youth of today. Think of it as a disguise.

They'd given me a picture of Ruth. A pocketsize high school senior photo of a smiling blonde with her whole future ahead of her. I slipped it into one of those plastic sheaths in my wallet. She was a freshman at Meramec Community College. No one had heard from her in two weeks. They were afraid she'd fallen in with bad company. Their words. They watch too much TV. The police had investigated Ruth's disappearance but since she was an adult and there was no evidence of foul play, they'd figured she'd just split for Hollywood or Haight-Ashbury, take your pick. They suggested the couple hire a private detective. One of the few friends I still had on the force gave them my number.

Traffic started to thin out. This part of downtown would soon be as deserted as the face of the moon. Since the Birds had finished a dismal fourth in the newly formed Eastern Division, there was no series going on. I got up and headed to where I'd left my heap parked. A nine-year-old Studebaker built like a small tank. I called it the Beast. My landlord said it looked like three outhouses stuck together. It was an ugly car, especially with the rust and faded light brown paint. But it ran and got me where I wanted to go. Most of the time.

Grandma had told me Ruth was taking mostly theater classes and she liked to hang out in the campus coffeehouse with the rest of the artistic crowd. So, I fired the Beast up, tuned in to KSHE for some decent rock, and headed toward Kirkwood, stopping once at a White Castle for a quick dinner of belly bombers, fries, and a Coke. I'd be burping all evening.

The sun was setting by the time I reached the campus. Goodbye KSHE until tomorrow. MCC was one of a trio of junior colleges that had sprung up over the past decade. Located in the southeast corner of some massive, undeveloped wooded lot, at the intersection of Big Bend and Geyer, the college was gradually spreading west. The coffeehouse was located in one of the temporary barracks buildings slated for teardown as soon as more of the permanent brick and mortar institutes of higher learning were completed.

There were maybe a dozen people scattered about the room, students and a hip professor or two. I took a seat at a back table and watched through the heavy layer of stale cigarette smoke as some Gaslight Square wannabe recited really bad poetry. Man, he sucked. Would fit right in on what was left of the Square.

After a while a waitress wandered over and asked if I wanted anything. I glanced at a chalkboard menu set in the corner, couldn't decipher any of it and told her to bring me a regular coffee, black. Just what I needed on top of my dinner. On stage, Ovid began strumming a guitar to accompany his babble.

The waitress returned with my drink. "Excuse me," I said and flipped open my wallet to Ruth's picture. "Do you know her by any chance?"

She took my wallet, held the photo close to her face, and squinted at it in the dim light, while I took a sip of over brewed muck. "You The Man?" she said looking back at me.

"Do I look like fuzz?" She shrugged. "I'm her older brother," I lied. "No one's seen her in a couple of weeks. Family's getting worried, afraid she split for San Fran or somewhere."

"She never said anything about an older brother."

So, she did know her. "I'm sort of the black sheep of the family. You dig?"

"Yeah, I can dig it. Sure, I know Ruth but I ain't seen her in a while." Obviously, my waitress wasn't an English major.

"You know where she might be?"

"Have you tried Rainy Daze? I heard she had a job there, working with the light show or something. She's big into the theater. Wants to be an actress or director. But you'd know that, as her brother."

"Yeah, it's like an obsession. Thanks," I laid a buck on the table. "Keep the change."

Rainy Daze was out in the boonies, along Olive Street at Old Hog Hollow Rd. I rolled off the college lot and crossed Big Bend to a filling station. The Beast guzzled gasoline like it was a kid hooked on Kool-Aid. I hopped out and opened the tank, self-service. Jesus Christ! Gas was up to thirty-seven cents a gallon. Did the damn oil companies think we were made of money? I filled the tank, paid, and popped in an eight-track tape, Grace Slick and the Jefferson Airplane. I took Big Bend to I-244, singing along to White Rabbit. I-244 was open now all the way from I-44 to I-70. Dual highway, two lanes each way. Maybe someday they'd get it completed.

Exiting at Olive, I crossed the interstate and headed out on the narrow, winding two-lane road. It was darker than the nether reaches of Hades out here. No streetlights, no traffic lights, no traffic. It was like I'd just entered the Twilight Zone or something. The first lights I saw were on the Daze's parking lot. The lot looked full with several cars parked along the shoulder. Must have a good act tonight. I pulled off in front of the last car, managed not to go into the ditch, and hiked back. I noted a trio of customized bikes on the lot, ape-hanger handlebars, extended front forks, sissy bars.

I went into the lobby. There was a pool table there and the three biker types were shooting pool. They were members of The Devils MC, whoever or whatever that was. Not good. The owner would be well advised to run them off.

I went up to the snack bar and asked the kid working there if the manager was in. I had to shout to be heard over the music coming from the auditorium.

"Don't know," he said.

"How about Ruth?"

"Who?"

"Ruth."

"Ruth who?"

"Ruth Parker."

"Don't know."

"What do you know?"

"Huh?"

"Never mind." I left Mr. Encyclopedia Brittanica and went to the main entrance, paid the fee, got the back of my hand stamped, and went inside. The building had once been a warehouse or large garage or something or another. The stage room was huge and packed with groups of teenyboppers and horny boys. Mostly empty tables sat along the walls. The music was deafening. Some rock group out of Chicago. One long-haired, bare-chested virtuoso stood in front of the rest of the band playing an electric violin while a psychedelic light show lit up the wall behind them.

Okay, that was pretty cool.

I found the stairs that led up to the control booth and slipped up them. The door to the booth was locked. I rattled it, then knocked on it.

"Go away!" came a female voice.

"Hey, just want to talk to you for a minute, okay?"

"I'm busy. Piss off before I call security!"

They have security here? Figuring I wouldn't get anywhere this way, I went back down to the main floor, found empty wall space nearby, leaned into it, and crossed my arms. Sooner or later the band would take a break. I occupied my time ogling all the hot chicks. College girls along with jailbait dressed in mini-skirts, bell bottoms, granny dresses, tight jeans. Nobody danced. The audience just stood in a tight-packed mob in front of the stage and kissed their hearing goodbye.

After several songs, the band did take a break. I watched the restrooms fill up. I heard a door unlock and then steps on the stairs. A gorgeous, late-twenties, redheaded babe, dressed in jeans and tie-dyed top hurried down the steps. I stepped in front of her. "Hey," I said.

"You the asshole who was knocking on my door?" she said.

"Guilty. I'd like to ask you a few questions." I held up a bill with the likeness of Alexander Hamilton on it. "For five minutes of your time."

She snatched the bill from my hand and motioned for me to follow her. She led me into an office and shut the door behind us. "Gotta pee first," she said and disappeared through another door. After a couple of minutes, I heard a toilet flush, a faucet run and then she was back. "Make it fast, I gotta get back."

"I'm looking for my sister, Ruth Parker."

"Aren't we all."

"I was told she works here. In the light booth."

"She's supposed to, but she hasn't shown tonight."

"Any idea where she might be."

She shrugged. Then noticing my scowl said, "Those bikers still out front?"

"Devils MC?"

"Yeah. She's kind of taken up with one of them."

"Those dirtbags?"

"There's a young one, sort of cute. Lou something or another. I think he's trying to get into their club. The others pretty much treat him like a gofer. Haven't seen him in a week or so either. Warned her to stay away from him. But kids don't listen. Think trash like that is groovy. Talk to Rat, he might help you."

"Which one's Rat? They all look ratty to me."

"If he's there, you won't have any trouble recognizing him. Now, I need to get back."

I wandered back to the lobby. There was a lot of foot traffic through the room. The bikers were still shooting pool. I found a space by a wall where I could pretend to watch the game while I studied them. Rat was easy to spot. Imagine a rat in a pair of oil-stained jeans, boots, dirty tee, and Levi vest that sported the club colors, and you got him. Rat had a long, pointed nose fittingly enough, but instead of whiskers he'd grown a nasty thin stash, furry patch under his lower lip, and a scraggly goatee. The other two Hells Angels wannabes were bigger, hairier, and dumber looking. I'd bet their combined IQs didn't add up to the outdoor temperature.

What were these thugs doing here anyway? The drinking age in Missouri stands at twenty-one. No booze was sold here. It was a teen hangout for high school and JC kids. It didn't take long to clear that question up. A teenage boy, trying hard to look hip, strolled up and said something to Rat. The biker put down his cue and they left by the front door. After a few minutes Rat was back, picked up his cue and resumed the game. They were pushing drugs. Gee, what a surprise.

What else did outlaw bikers do? White slavery? I felt heat flash through my body and my muscles tense. Ruth, you silly fool. Groovy, my ass. These guys were scum. Rat left to use the pay phone. When he got back, one of his partners said, "You talk to the kid?"

Rat nodded. "Roxton wants her brought to the Courts on Watson, at one, after things quiet down. I'll handle it. She's gonna get her starring role," he said with a greasy smirk. The other two laughed.

Watson Road, courts, Coral Courts. But was she Ruth? And what's a starring role? I noticed one of the thugs stare at me. I could see the rusty wheels start to spin inside his cranium like 'what was this cat doing eyeballing us?' I slipped Ruth's photo out of my wallet, stepped over next to Rat who had bent over the table to line up a shot, and laid it on the felt next to his cue. He glanced at it, said, "Cute chick," and went on with his shot, sinking a stripe in the far corner pocket. He stood and chalked his stick. "Looking for your daughter, man? Or you horny for a Lolita to bang?" His buddies laughed.

"She's my sister."

"No shit," he said, brushed past me and sunk another stripe.

"Her name is Ruth Parker," I said. "She's a freshman at Meramec." He shrugged, but Dumb and Dumber weren't as cool. Dumber's eyes opened wide and he glanced at Dumb who tried to give him an ix-nay sign with his hand.

Rat caught it too, laid down his cue, and said to his buddies, "Be right back." He nodded for me to follow him outside.

I followed out the front door and around to the back of the lot where the employees parked. He turned and stared at me for several moments. One of the problems of dealing with dummies is it tends to make you do dumb things too, like believing his buds would wait inside for him. I heard a footstep behind me with just enough time to duck and get the pool cue across my back instead of my noggin. The blow knocked me to the ground and before I could get up, I had three pairs of boots kicking and stomping me. I tucked my head and curled into a ball.

An ear-splitting siren cut loose, and a bright light lit up the lot.

"Pigs!" one of the bikers yelled. The three scrambled away. A few moments later I heard their bikes fire up and roar off. A car door opened. I rolled onto my back and watched the redheaded light show director walk over, backlit by a car spotlight. "You're not too bright, are you?" she said.

"Guess not," I said and sat up. My back ached and my ribs hurt. She lowered a hand and tugged me to my feet. "Thought you had a light show to run."

"I figured you'd probably do something stupid, so I let one of the kids fill in."

I followed her over to her car, a black Ford Custom 500. She reached in, turned the spotlight off, and locked the door. "Surplus police car?"

She nodded. "Bought off the lot with the spot on it, but I had to have the siren added. Comes in handy from time to time. Good way to clear a parking lot after dark. Fire up the siren, flash the spot, and people split quick. C'mon."

I followed her through a back door and to the office where she let me wash up in the private john. She was at the desk, smoking, when I came back in. "So, who are you? Ruth told me she was an only child, raised by her grandparents. Her mom and dad were killed in a car wreck when she was two."

"I'm a private investigator, Kevin Mann. Ruth's grandparents hired me to find her."

"I hope they aren't paying you."

"Okay, I got careless out there, but I think I got a lead on her. Ever hear of a movie director, Roxton?"

"No. Should I have?"

I shrugged and glanced around the cluttered office. Photos of several different groups and performers hung on the walls. "Are you the manager here?"

She shook her head. "No. They hire me to put on the light shows just like they hire the bands to play. I got my own business."

"You know those bikers are pushing drugs."

"Damn it," she said and sighed. "I was afraid of that. I know they've been told to stay away but they don't. Can't call The Man on them. The fuzz bust them here, they'll use that as an excuse to shut the club down. Then where will the kids go?"

Good question, for which I had no answer.

After a brief pause, she snuffed out her cigarette and stood. "I need to get back before that kid screws up the works." She stopped by the door and held it open. "I hope you find Ruth."

"Oh, I will. You can count on it," I said in my best PI voice. Peter Gunn couldn't have done any better. I nodded, left the office and started down the hall.

"Hey, Kevin," she called at my back. I turned around. "I'm Rhonda by the way. Stop by some night when you're not working. I'll buy you a Coke," she said and smiled.

I resisted the urge to say, sure thing, doll. Mike Hammer didn't play too well with women anymore. "I'll do that," I said instead.

Outside the night had gotten chilly. My watch read just after ten. I fired up the Beast, managed a U-turn, and headed back to the interstate. The Coral Courts were one of a bunch of no-tell motels located along Watson Road, old Route 66, in Marlborough. If I had a reason to believe a crime was going to be committed, I sort of had a duty to notify the local heat. I wasn't sure the Marlborough cops could handle anything tougher than writing speed trap tickets. Did I really know that a crime was imminent? I convinced myself that I didn't.

Getting beat up always makes me hungry, so I stopped at a Shakey's and got a small sausage, pepperoni, and extra cheese pizza to go. Then I hit a 7-11 for a quart bottle of Falstaff and motored onto the Courts.

The Coral Courts were built in the forties in Art Deco style. Cute curvy bungalows constructed from yellow-glazed bricks and glass blocks, each with its own attached garage. I'd been here a couple of times before with my Polaroid, hunting straying spouses. I just can't seem to stay away from motels like this no matter what the job was.

I stopped at the office and told the slimy looking clerk that I wanted a room for the night.

"The entire night?" he said.

"Yeah, my old lady kicked me out."

"You alone? Got company coming?"

"Yes, I'm alone. No, no company coming."

"Looking for some company?"

"I'm looking for a good night's sleep. So, give me one of the rooms in the back."

"No need to get testy," he said and handed me a key. "Want to keep our customers happy so they'll come back."

"Right." I paid, drove to the appropriate cottage, and eased the Beast into the garage. It was a tight fit. The damn car was so long I couldn't close the garage door. I went inside, ate the pizza and guzzled the beer, while I planned out my strategy. There really wasn't much of a plan to make. I'd determine what room they used to film the porno, bust in, and do my Jim Dandy to the rescue bit. I hoped she wanted to be rescued.

I should have gotten a second bottle of Falstaff. What was I thinking? I didn't even carry a gun. What kind of PI doesn't pack a rod? Sherlock Holmes? The kind that wants to stay out of jail, I told myself. Gunplay looks cool on TV where the good guy never misses, never fails to shoot the gun out of the bad guy's hand. Never hits an innocent bystander by mistake. Things aren't that clean in real life. Guns had consequences that were seldom good.

Along about midnight, I turned off the lights, and went outside. I got a dark-blue windbreaker and a black knit cap out of my trunk along with a five-cell flashlight. I moved over into the woods that bordered the lot and found a good vantage point. It was getting colder but at least I wouldn't have to worry about any mosquitoes. I lay down on a bed of fallen leaves by the tree with the largest trunk.

At twelve-thirty, a white van pulled up to a nearby bungalow. Two men got out and started carrying floodlights, stands, a camera, a microphone and heavy blackout curtains inside. I watched the lights disappear as the curtains were hung up then moved in closer. Just before one, two bikes roared onto the lot. Rat was riding one and a younger guy, packing a woman behind him, was on the other. They stopped, killed their engines, and dismounted. Even in the dim light I could see the girl was a blonde and matched Ruth's physique. I could also see she wasn't overly pleased to be here.

"I don't know, Lou," she said. "I'm not sure I want to do this."

"Ah, baby, it'll be fine," Lou said. "We'll shoot a couple of films and make some real bread."

"I don't know," she said again.

"C'mon!" Rat said. "Get inside."

Lou put his arm around Ruth's shoulders and led her inside. He continued to feed her a line of lovey-dovey BS. A shaft of bright light spilled out onto the parking lot but was quickly extinguished by the closing door. I waited a few minutes to make sure they weren't coming back out and then scampered over. I could hear more arguing going on inside. Apparently, director Roxton wasn't too pleased to find he had a reluctant leading lady. Rat yelled to get the rest of her clothes off.

I eased inside, where the lights were almost blinding. Ruth sat on the bed against the headboard, legs tucked under her, clad only in bra and panties. She'd wrapped her arms around her chest. Lou sat on the bed next to her wearing only his jeans. "C'mon baby," he said while he tried to unfasten her bra. "It'll be fun. We'll make a groovy movie."

"No! I don't want to do this!" she said and pushed him away.

"Hell with it! Strip her!" Rat ordered.

"Hey, jerkwater," I said. "She said she doesn't want to."

Rat spun around toward me. I drove the handle of the five-cell flashlight into his gut as hard as I could. He let out a whoosh of air and crumpled to the floor. Lou hopped off the bed and pulled out a switchblade.

"You really don't want to do that, kid," I said. He tried to lunge at me, but his feet got tangled in his discarded clothes. I easily dodged his thrust and smashed the large end of the flashlight against his wrist. The knife fell to the floor and he collapsed next to the bed screaming. He cradled his injured wrist in his other hand and glared at me.

"Stay put, sonny." I glanced at Ruth. "Get dressed."

"Who the hell do you think you are, interrupting my shoot?" It was director Roxton who could have been Rat's doppelganger. Same scrawny physique, same shoestring moustache, except he was dressed all in black, including a black beret.

"I'm with the Hollywood Screen Censor board," I said. "I'm shutting you down."

"Wise guy, huh? You know who I am?" he bellowed and puffed himself up.

"Yeah, I know who you are. You're a dirty little man who makes dirty movies."

"I am an arteest! My films they are art!" he said with a phony French accent he just remembered to use.

Geez, give me a break.

"And I have backers. They aren't going to like this when they hear about it."

"So, don't tell them."

"You weesh. They're not the type of people you want to mess with. Sort of a…" He paused to find the right word, "a worldwide corporation and—"

"A corporation, huh? How's their dental plan?"

"What?"

I punched him in the mouth with a right fist and he crumpled against a light stand, knocking it over. The light hit the floor, the bulb popped like a gunshot, and a whiff of smoke went up. He lay next to it, hand on his mouth and moaning.

I turned toward the last man in the room. He was another real winner. Mid-to late fifties, skinny, and wearing red pants with a white belt that matched his shoes and a paisley shirt. He had thinning cotton-colored hair he wore long and had a three-day growth of facial fuzz. "Hey, I'm just the cameraman," he said, stood back and raised his hands to shoulder level.

I nodded. "This your camera?" I pointed at the large contraption atop a tripod.

"Yes, it is."

"Expensive?"

"Damn expensive."

I nodded again, knelt, collapsed the camera stand's legs then stood and swung the camera against the wall like Babe Ruth laying into a high hard one. The camera exploded into a shower of sparks and pieces.

"Are you crazy?" He yelled and started toward me but stopped when I turned back to him. "Hey, I'm cool. I'm cool," he said, raised his hands again and eased back.

Ruth, seated on the edge of the bed, had finished dressing, and was tying her sneakers. I took hold of her hand and led her to the door. "Let's get out of here."

Our path led us past Rat, who was on his knees but still bent over, holding his middle. "You're a dead man," he said.

I hunkered down next to him where our faces would be on the same level. "Oh, yeah? And who's going to make me that way? That gang of brainless morons you ride with? Bring 'em on. Besides, you got a bigger problem." I snagged the bottom of his vest, tore it off him, and dangled it in front of his face. "What do you think they're going to say when you tell them you lost your biker cut?"

"You—you bastard. Give it back."

"No. And while you're trying to explain that away, tell that pack of turds to stay away from Rainy Daze and all the rest of the teen hangouts. Or I'll start making a collection of these rags." I led Ruth outside and then just for orneriness, tipped over both bikes. They landed on the concrete drive with a satisfying crunch.

Ruth was shivering so I draped my windbreaker around her and led her back to the room I'd rented. I didn't bother going in, just tossed the key down by the front door, loaded her into the Beast and backed out. We rolled off the lot and headed for her grandparents' house. She'd curled up against the far door and tried to fight off tears.

"He… he told me he loved me. That I was beautiful, and he wanted to marry me," she said through the sniffles. "Then he wanted us to have sex while that man filmed it. With Rat too. I—I feel so ashamed," She burst into tears.

"True love," I said, reached over the backrest, snagged a box of tissues from the backseat, and handed them to her. I stopped at a payphone to call her grandparents, figuring that would cause less of a stir than beating on their front door at two in the morning. All the downstairs lights were on when I pulled to a stop. I got Ruth out and grandma met us on the front porch. There was a lot of crying, hugging, and apologizing. They clasped each other tight and stumbled down the hallway to the kitchen, I suppose.

Grandpa led me into the parlor. "Where did you find her?" he said.

"Somewhere she had no business being. Like you feared, she fell in with bad company. I think she learned her lesson." I was too tired to add up my expenses, so I told him to pay me for two days work and we'd call it even. He sat down at an old rolltop desk and wrote out a check for two-hundred bucks. I glanced around to see if he still had a hand-crank phone on a wall but didn't spot one. He handed me the check, shook my hand with a firm grip, and I took my leave.

Back in the Beast I fired it up but let it idle. I was beat and needed to crash for about twelve hours. It'd been quite a day. Two hundred was more than an honest patrolman made in a week. I might not be as smooth as the detectives on TV or in the novels, but I'd gotten the job done. The girl had been rescued and returned unharmed back to the bosom of her family. I'd met a pretty groovy chic too, Rhonda the redheaded light show babe. I intended to take her up on that offer of a Coke. Of course, I now had a biker gang after my skin, and maybe the mob as well.

Still, I felt a grin curl my lips. I let out a grunt of satisfaction. I couldn't help but think that somewhere Mike Hammer, Peter Gunn and Phillip Marlowe were shooting me a grin. Along with a tip of their hats.

Yeet the Writers

Eileen Dreyer

A lifelong St. Louisan, Eileen Dreyer remembers her grandfather teaching her how to keep score at a Cardinals' game when she was three years old. Now she's just taught her own grandsons. In between, she has enjoyed two careers—as a trauma nurse and New York Times bestselling author of a variety of romances and medical suspense, in which she kills off everybody who annoyed her when she worked her 'real' job. She's much nicer to her romance characters.

G. R. Miller

An active member of Sisters in Crime St. Louis, published author and poet currently developing two St. Louis-based crime-novel series. For a time, he lived in Colorado's Rocky Mountains, where lack of oxygen at altitude sparked enough creativity to inspire him to write. Life experiences and a vivid imagination ignite the characters and their ensuing tales into a debut novel and more.

Daniel Sohn

Born and raised in St Louis, Dan Sohn has ventured far but always returns. His career path arcs include computer services manager, math teacher, medical practice, and now author. For decades, journaling followed him on travels, parental adventures, and diversions. Wayward impulses still contribute to a zig-zaggy approach to life.

C. A. Fehmel

She has always lived in St. Louis, but still doesn't know her way around. She even got lost going to her own house three days after she bought it. She says it was 'unusually foggy' that night. Yeah, sure. Haunting cemeteries has always been one of her favorite pastimes. She encourages tourists to visit the huge and historical cemeteries of Bellefontaine and Calvary near the Mississippi River. She warns, be cautious if you hear suspicious noises.

Stormy White

A writer of mysteries and science fiction, she has lived in various states, employed in a variety of jobs. Her most exciting and stressful gig was as a defense attorney. While working as a St. Louis public defender, there were extraordinary highs and lows and many lessons. Two of which are that: everybody wants to win, and, that everybody lies. She began to volunteer at the St. Louis Zoo where folks avoid adversarial conflict, love the animals, and never send anyone to prison.

Sarahlynn Lester

Her family, along with a giant Saint Berdoodle puppy, live in St. Louis. Shep is definitely a St. Louis dog—Saint is right in his name, although he likes spelling it out. No abbreviations for him. His version of asking strangers where they went to high school is to jump up and put his paws on their shoulders to sniff out the information. When not being dragged around the block by Shep, Sarahlynn's written short stories and essays that have been published in apt literary magazines and anthologies. She also writes young adult novels. In her spare time, she is president of the St. Louis chapter of Sisters in Crime, and an active member of both the St. Louis Writers Guild and SCBWI. She attended high school Somewhere Else.

Catina Williams

A professor of psychology, she lives in St. Louis with her husband. She enjoys a passionate affair with writing and often cozies up with an old-fashioned notebook and pen. And perhaps a glass of wine. Catina blithely follows her muse into whatever genre or form the muse selects.

Vicki Erwin

Having spent more than one Fourth of July pregnant and with a toddler(s), sizzling in the heat under the Arch, she is more than qualified to write "Magpie Baby." It could have happened. She is a veteran of the book biz, has written over 30 books, worked as a sales rep for Scholastic, and owned a bookstore. She lives in a St. Louis suburb with her husband (and sometimes co-author) and their dog, Luna (never a co-author, obvious bias).

Glen Bush

A reformed English professor, who now lives in the Lake of the Ozarks, he writes crime noir and urban fiction, walks his crazy Aussie, Myloh, and travels with his family. A product of Old North St. Louis, a working-class neighborhood, his stories come from the people he knew. It was a neighborhood filled with good friends, beautiful women, small time criminals, hustlers, and hard-working blue-collar folks, city-bred and hoosiers both. Without these people, his stories would never have come to fruition.

Fedora Amis

A winner of the Mayhaven Prize for her book *Jack the Ripper in St. Louis,* she liked the experience so much, she wrote three more Victorian who-done-its. She learned what it's like to live without indoor plumbing—while wearing a girdle. With such a warped early life, could you be surprised at her quirky characters who won't quit and can't be quiet? Too lazy to read an ebook or hard copy? Ain't we all? So, listen to Fedora narrate her audiobook instead. She gets to mention her book's title because, well, her editor is afraid of what might happen otherwise.

JD Frain

He's on record as supposedly having more flaws than any of his characters, yet he continues to work on his debut novel anyway. He is a graduate of the University of Missouri School of Journalism, and his short fiction has been featured in *Ellery Queen Mystery Magazine, Flash Bang Mysteries, The Twin Bill* and wherever they'll have him. For a little suspense and a little more laughter, he also writes flash fiction.

Larry Lovan

Having spent most of his life slaving away in Corporate America. Twelve years ago, he hit his Popeye point—"That's all I can standz, I can't standz no more." He retired and decided to spend the rest of his days writing. Agents, publishers, his wife, all told him no one's interested in outlaw bikers, Woodstock, or the American Civil War. They were wrong. All of them.